Asherah

Brian Smith

Foreword

I was on my way to work mid-September 2013 when a friend called from out of state. He and I were both police officers in a northern Colorado city and he was on vacation. He asked if I was busy and what the status of our community was. I laughed and asked why he would be concerned about the status of the city. He explained the news had been showing images of flooding along the northern front range and the negative impact many communities were experiencing. Looking out the windows of my car, I told him it was cloudy and gray and only sprinkling. It would be hard to believe there was much flooding given what I was witnessing. I assured him the news was probably exaggerating to get its audience to watch but told him I would keep him posted.

Pulling into the parking lot at the PD I noticed more cars than usual. My office was in the administration side of the building and as I walked upstairs, I immediately noticed the Emergency Operations Center (EOC) was in full swing. I hurried down the hall and saw all the TVs were on and the news was, indeed, speaking of region-wide flooding. Asking around was futile as everyone was busy, but I was able to determine there was a serious threat to our city. Unsure how to help, I started making coffee. This was also a ruse to stay in the room and listen in on how bad things were. This was my hometown, and I had a vested interest both professionally and personally.

Finding one of my supervisors, I told him I was ready to put aside my administrative work, don my uniform, and do anything I could to help. Not recognizing the reality of how bad it was going to be, he told me things were under control and I should just stay in my office. I sauntered back to my closet-turned-office and listened to the police radio. It was immediately clear to me how bad things were and how much worse they may get. Officers were unable to keep up with the surging water, evacuations, and road closures.

I ignored my sergeant, put on my uniform, grabbed a patrol car, and went into service. For the next several days, my co-workers and I worked 15 or more hours a day trying to keep the city safe, which was a daunting task given the severity of the storm. Some friends of mine were working even while their homes were destroyed by the floods. Their strength and resolve were emotional to watch. The community rallied together as best we could, but the storm ravaged many homes and destroyed memories stored in boxes on lower levels. My family didn't see me for several days, as I was geographically cut off from them due to the floods covering major highways.

Even as the water subsided, the recovery continued for months and years. Driving through neighborhoods and watching people sift through garbage to find pictures was devastating. What mementos and photos they did find, were hung carefully to air dry and hopefully be salvaged. So much was lost.

This book is a tribute to the people who served, those who lost, and those who chose to thrive afterward. Being enmeshed in my community hours upon hours was emotionally draining, yet very rewarding. I watched as people unhooked their boats from trailers in their driveways and used them to save their neighbors and their pets. There was not one person who fathomed they would be performing boat rescues in their own land-locked neighborhoods. Many heroes arose during this difficult storm.

While this book is most certainly a work of fiction, had it not been for that storm, I would not have thought of this plot. What you will read is an accounting of what I witnessed and what I later imagined as a pretty cool story. I tried to stick to historical facts throughout, while mixing in fantasy.

This book is dedicated to the families that lost so much and the hundreds of people from local, state, and federal agencies that arose to the *challenge to rescue and protect so many communities during an unprecedented event, later referred to as the 500-year flood.*

June 28, 1847

Where the plains and foothills of the Rocky Mountains merge

"What have you done?!" Weston hollered at Lady O'Kayo. The elderly sage had promised him prosperity, but her evil and vile magic had summoned a nightmare rather than fortune.

"I have done only what you inquired of me. You wanted rain. It's yours to have." Her words were slow and drawn out.

"This isn't what I wanted! I needed to feed my family. The drought was killing my crops."

"And now you will have rain, and your family will have food. But such requests come at a price."

Lady O'Kayo's scraggly voice was in stark contrast to the intensifying screams of the monster she created. Weston smashed his hands hard against his ears hoping to squelch the noise. He watched in horror as the tattered leg of a deer was tossed into the air after the creature voraciously ripped its prey apart.

"Take it back! Please." Weston's voice cracked as he fell to his knees begging Lady O'Kayo to reverse what she had done. He raised his hands toward her in a prayerful position, his eyes pleading for her to undue this horror.

"It is too late, Weston. I warned you against such greed," she replied with a faint smile.

The drought had lasted five weeks, but tonight the storm clouds clapped with thunder as Lady O'Kayo looked into the blackened sky and raised her hands in homage to the falling rain. Weston realized his lust for protection cost more than he imagined. He could not overturn what she had done, but he would make sure no one knew the cause of this nightmare. Weston arose from his knees and drew his revolver from its holster. As Lady O'Kayo leveled her gaze to meet his, Weston raised the pistol and pulled the trigger. The bullet hit its target, and the woman fell to the ground with a hole replacing where her right eye once peered into his soul. Weston anticipated the beast would die with the one who conjured it from the earth. Instead, her death fed its appetite. Weston had killed his one protector.

He turned to run but was no match for its speed. Weston only ran a few steps before he was pushed to the ground. The revolver was still in his right hand, and he maneuvered his body to take aim at the monster. He shot off only one bullet before the beast pushed its full weight upon Weston's stomach. The bulk of this thing now sitting atop Weston slowly forced air out of his lungs. Weston gasped for breath. He helplessly flailed his arms at the furry demon but lost all strength with the deprivation of oxygen. As Weston's flesh was pulled from his bones, his mind screamed in prayer; something he should have done before this day began.

September 12, 2013 - 8:00AM
Bekkett, Colorado

The morning forecast called for cool, rainy weather. This annoyed Marie Corintho because she had a meticulously scheduled day, and this prediction of moisture was not part of her plan. For Marie, it was more than a mere inconvenience of rain; such weather patterns sparked a tremble of anxiety within. When Marie was a young girl, her free-spirited parents, Joe and Sheri, often enjoyed evenings with their friends. The group of adults sat around the oval kitchen table playing cards or a variety of board games. As they waited for their turn, they bantered about life and the happenings around town. They also enjoyed wine and beer, causing the volume of their voices to increase with their inebriation.

It was usually under the influence of their choice of drinks the conversation took a turn toward recalling tales of the mysterious beast roaming the countryside just outside town. The vivacious tales of a ferocious animal that only appeared during storms always turned gruesome. The adults would find themselves increasing their tone and getting carried away with gory details, quickly followed by hushes and awkward glances in Marie's direction.

Sitting on the floor in the adjacent room, Marie would quietly pretend to focus on her coloring book. She was rarely coloring with any degree of care. Her curiosity at the tales had her acting as though her parents' loud voices fell on deaf ears. Instead, she listened intently and was both intrigued and terrified by the stories she heard. The words became emblazoned in her mind during all those times she mindlessly scratched colors onto a black and white page as a kid, while silently absorbing the tales of the adults.

Over the course of her youth listening to the stories, Marie gained very little information of value. Most of the verbosity of the adults seemed to be nothing more than passed-down fairy tales. Still, her parents and their friends seemed to believe this animal they often called the Bekkett Beast was a creature possessing extreme terror that came alive during rainstorms. As they recounted, the storm resurrected the beast from the grave with its one mission to hunt and eat its prey. The adults blathered on claiming that both people and animals alike were feasted upon. At the conclusion of each re-telling, Sheri would laugh at how preposterous the notion was and wondered what would motivate someone to create such a story. While the proof of its existence was always in question, an eight-year-old girl can carry quite the imagination, and Marie carried the possibility of truth with her as she grew up.

Now, staring blankly at the window, Marie's mind was thrust back to the present. She noticed her reflection in the glass and saw her glossed over eyes. "Humph," she grunted out loud as her body involuntarily shook. Despite her uncertainty of the tales, rain always brought a chill to her bones – both literally and psychologically. As a twenty-three-year-old woman living on her own, she hated to admit her fears, but they were still with her. Reflecting on her past, she knew it was those weekend nights sitting on the floor in her family room that prompted her on-going search for the truth of the Bekkett Beast.

Turning away from the window and walking across the room in her small apartment, she announced sullenly, "How do weather forecasters live with themselves? Two days ago, they said it would be sunny today. Argh!"

Checking the weather at all was an oddity for Marie since Colorado was known to be unpredictable. Televised forecasts were mere words and cute animations that were only relevant during active blizzards. Mother Nature changed at her own choosing with no consideration or discussion with those who had already made plans. People were often seen huddling under shelters instead of basking in the sun. Many wedding parties had disastrous detours with the sudden onset of rain, snow, or wind.

Marie simply would not allow the possibility of rain to dampen her spirit. Instead, she chose to believe her appointment with Betty Bekkett would not be interrupted today. She had made arrangements with Betty weeks prior, and Marie needed this meeting to occur. She hoped it would provide her with culminating evidence to complete her research project. Betty was the sole proprietor of the Double K Ranch. Every other family member had either died or fled town years earlier. Betty was no spring-chicken and Marie needed to meet with her before something happened to Betty, possibly ending the Bekkett reign in this region. Marie knew going to the ranch today would not necessarily bring closure to her search for the beast, but she hoped Betty would trust Marie enough to pass on the truth or confirm it to be only a tale. Glancing through the window and seeing the grey clouds beginning to sweep over the mountain peaks, Marie silently wondered if this weather was an omen or just a mere coincidence.

***

The Town of Bekkett was Marie's home, and she enjoyed its quaint tranquility. The town was charmingly nestled near the foothills of the Rocky Mountains. It was north of Denver by just enough of a commute many people living and visiting the region did not want to stay. The population had grown over the years but capped at about 25,000 people. Most residents of Bekkett were happy to keep the growth at bay. There were too many nearby communities that lost their charm with the sudden growth from invading outsiders. Bekkett was happy to remain its own destination for the long timers who chose to stay within its borders.

Calmly meandering through the center of town was Sand Creek. Its location allowed those who enjoyed exercise to run, jog or bike along the miles-long trail the town built beside the creek's banks. It had been aptly named eons ago because it displayed its distended belly, the sandy bottom, more often than the once-a-year mountain runoff was able to cover. The sand below and bordering the creek created its namesake.

After graduating high school, Marie moved to Denver to obtain her degree in Western America Historical Studies. The Mile High City was a buzz of nightlife activity, but Marie's passions did not rely on bars, booze, or boys. She enjoyed humble research. She spent most weekends within the hallowed walls of the university library. Her time in Denver was necessary, but she quickly recognized her future was better suited in a smaller environment. She wanted to be away from the noise and distractions a large city openly offers.

After earning her bachelor's degree, Marie returned to Bekkett's peaceful solitude. Her introverted spirit kept her sane as she spent hours in the quiet corners of the library with her tedious research. Many people do not understand the motivations of the introverted soul. The introvert does not dislike people. On the contrary, they hope for the best in others. Introverts just do not need to revel in each and every detail being openly shared. Distant understanding of others was preferred.

It was this seclusive spirit that helped Marie thrive in her passionate hobby. Unlike so many others who thought historical research to be mundane, boring, and utterly useless, Marie found it to be joyful. She had uncovered stories of sojourners passing through the region. She learned of families struggling in the heat of eastern Colorado as they desperately sought the promise of gold in the mountains. She appreciated the ingenuity of settlers who left their possessions and moved west for land and wealth. A vast array of stories so many others thought to be worthless and carelessly tossed aside. She could not understand the carelessness of those who failed to admire and learn from their past.

Admittedly, some of her discoveries were ultimately futile facts. Even she found herself unconcerned about headlines in newspapers of yore hailing the arrival of a family from Denver. She could not understand why eating dinner with one's relatives was worthy to be documented in the news. Yet, she held onto the information she gleaned as bits of understanding into souls gone by. Souls she may someday meet upon her death. To be able to, on the other side of this life, introduce herself to those souls and reminisce with them still meant so much to Marie.

In her two years since returning from college, Marie's daily mission focused on uncovering the mystery of the fabled beast. This was not a new task for her. Since she was a young teen, she had hoped to discover the story behind the tales she had heard for so long. But in a small town like Bekkett, a young girl asking too many questions about a myth was generally met with laughter and a stern warning to "Let it go, honey." The gruesome accounts of bloodied livestock and missing pets seemed to conclude in the late 1800's. As the town modernized, the stories of the beast faded. The older generation of Bekkett were satisfied to let the stories put themselves to bed. But Marie could not shake the idea there was more to unearth. She had been meticulously writing down each narrative hoping to one day put the pieces of this mystery together.

***

Marie lived in a one-bedroom apartment complete with a combination living room-kitchen. It was not much, but she did not require more space for only herself and her research. Over the years, the information she gathered became pieces of evidence she cataloged in her small apartment. Unfortunately, she was no field researcher, and she did not enjoy roaming the land trying to find puzzle pieces. Her evidence collection came to her from the words on pages she pored over. Marie's analytical mind and ability to remember facts allowed her to read and store the information in her head or on the pages of her journal. Meeting

Betty Bekkett was as much field research as she liked to complete. She enjoyed getting to meet real-life humans who have lived or known those who lived in the era she was researching.

Recognizing her inability to accomplish much outside the walls of a library, she decided to hire someone to help her find the truth. To say she hired someone was a bit of a stretch as she had no financial means to pay another person. It was more along the lines of begging and pleading – just done with class to dissuade the appearance of desperation. Gavin Rossiter was, in fact, no detective. However, he did have connections to the resources and respect of the community, which Marie did not possess.

When Gavin's dad, Tom, retired from the Bekkett Police Department he began doing investigative work for insurance companies. As a result, Gavin became cheap labor for his dad and gained some experience in uncovering the truth and pushing aside lies. That was exactly the skill set Marie needed. She did not know how much experience he really brought to the table, she just knew it was more than she could offer. The only hitch to Marie's plan was Gavin's unwillingness to put what he claimed were "important assignments" aside to assist her pro bono. In addition to helping his dad, Gavin also worked investigative journalism for the Bekkett Gazette. Marie wondered how many newsworthy investigative stories there really were in this lazy town. But Gavin insisted he would not put his life on hold to chase down whatever she may demand. Marie was fairly certain he was only helping her because he really did not have any other jobs right now, despite his insistence he was a busy man.

***

Marie turned her attention back to her morning plans. She gathered her journal, purse, and car keys and headed outside. The sky was a light shade of gray and the clouds concealed the sun. It was not yet raining, and Marie took this as a good sign things would go her way. Marie unlocked her car, sat in the driver's seat, and placed her belongings in the empty seat beside her. She drew in a deep breath, excited for what her day may discover. As she slowly let out the air from her lungs, Marie put the car in drive and headed toward the Double K Ranch.

As Marie drove her decade-old Ford Focus down the country road, she reminisced about her days learning to drive on these dirt roads in this very vehicle. Most roads in this region were a boring east and west or north and south route. This was one of her favorite country roads because of its ups and downs and unexpected curves. It was not just a unique route to drive. It was also a reflection of her life.

***

Until she was ten years old, Marie lived a joyous life with her mom and dad, both philanthropists at heart, not in their banking account. The kindness Joe and Sheri exuded was displayed by constantly searching for problems to solve and people to save. Their generous attitude was admirable to such a young, impressionable girl. So much so, that on Marie's tenth birthday, she chose to forgo any gifts for herself. Instead, she asked her parents to take her to a homeless shelter where she could serve others lunch and help the shelter organize food boxes. The two-hour drive to Denver was filled with anticipation as Marie envisioned so many people benefiting from her willingness to sacrifice her own needs for those of others.

Volunteering at the Denver Rescue Mission was better than she had imagined. That morning, she packed boxed lunches that would be distributed to those who could not make it to the shelter on their own. As she loaded sandwiches into boxes, several residents of the shelter sat with Marie and talked about what led them to such dire straits. At the time, Marie did not consciously recognize the passion it stirred within her. She listened to the stories of the adults surrounding her, enraptured in the history they brought to life. As they spoke of choices their grandparents and parents made, Marie recognized how ancestral decisions have generational impacts. Without ill-will or sorrow, the people Marie came to serve hungrily fed her appetite for research. Her career path of study began as she sat in a back room of a homeless shelter listening to the ventures of those less fortunate than herself.

Marie's tenth birthday was not just a lesson in serving others and realizing the differences among people; it was also one of the last memories she had of her parents. The following week, Marie's parents said a brief goodbye and assured her they would be home for dinner that evening. With a kiss on the cheek, her mom said they were going to be gone for the afternoon to help a couple who were about to be evicted from their family's land. Marie loved her parents' enthusiasm to help others and said she would have macaroni and cheese ready for dinner when they returned. Joe and Sheri pulled out of the driveway and waved goodbye as they drove toward the mountains. It was the last goodbye she gave her parents.

Evening came with no word from her mom or dad. By the next morning, Marie knew something awful had happened. To assuage her pain, Marie often envisioned her parents somewhere in the world making it a better place. She prayed they were pouring their selfless hearts into those who possessed so little themselves. She hoped their journey to the mountains had been their gentle way of telling her goodbye, knowing they needed to do more in the world than they could accomplish in Bekkett. Marie wished her parents had found the ultimate mission to accomplish, however, she also knew they would never leave her out of selfish ambition.

Two days after her parent's disappearance, Marie moved in with her eccentric grandmother. Not even her peculiar sayings and boisterous laugh could cover the sorrow overtaking Marie's body. She cried herself to sleep at night and would stare longingly at the mountains during the day. Pain followed her down every street reminding her of evening walks holding her mother's hand. Marie spiraled into isolation. The peace her parents had brought so many others, ended up bringing her the opposite. Marie was left with only her memories.

Her hopes that her parents were living and serving others in a better life ended two years later. A developer began clearing trees for a home site in the mountains and discovered a gruesome sight. Her parent's bodies, decomposed and mostly unrecognizable, were located. The authorities suspected her parents had been savagely beaten and left to die in a desolate mountain cabin. Police surmised the couple her parents had intended to help had other plans. The money, little as it was, they brought to help the young couple was never located and the police suspected robbery as a motive. Her parents' death, while she was so young, fueled her motivation to live in the past via research.

When Marie left for college, she swore she would never return to Bekkett; the place that took her life away. Marie poured herself into academics. Books befriended her like long-lost lovers. She cherished each new historical discovery. Her research of ancient stories and mysteries provided deep satisfaction into a soul that had little joy. Upon graduation, with only her grandmother to cheer her on, Marie decided she could not run from her past. Marie returned to Bekkett where the one mystery that had haunted her for years was still awaiting an answer.

She wondered how many other children lost those they loved because of the Bekkett Beast. How many souls ached as Marie's did when the person they most cared about never came home? Marie knew she had to unravel this secret, which is why she was traveling down this dusty road to the Double K Ranch today.

September 12, 2013 – 9:30AM

As the windshield wipers swept away the rain dotted window, Marie's memories were also pushed aside when she realized she had driven past Betty Bekkett's property. Making a U-turn on this narrow road was not going to be easy. After one futile attempt at turning around, Marie put the car in reverse and hoped she could navigate a half mile using only the rear window. She slowed the car as the front tires reached the driveway, stopped, then put the car back in its rightful forward gear. Marie turned left and followed the winding driveway a quarter mile off the roadway. The curvy, tree-lined lane dropped in elevation to where the main house sat along the banks of Sand Creek.

Marie stepped out of the car and was thankful for the covering of trees blocking much of the rain that had started to fall during her drive to the ranch. In her haste to leave the house, she left her umbrella by the front door. She hoped it was not a warning of just how much rain was to come. Marie hustled to the front door and lightly rapped on its window. She did not want to startle the elderly woman who graciously invited Marie into a realm so few were willing to acknowledge existed. Along with the tales of the Bekkett Beast came the loathing of the family whose name it bore.

Betty answered and looked startled. "Oh, dear. I was sure the rain would keep you at bay, honey. I wasn't expecting you."

"Nothing short of a flood would keep me from this meeting!" Even as Marie uttered the words, she realized they were probably not appropriate, given how close to the swollen waters of the creek Betty's house sat. Looking over her shoulder at the creek, Marie said, "I'm sorry. That was an insensitive thing to say."

"Think nothing of it, dear. Those banks haven't been breached by water throughout the entire history of this ranch. It's not going to happen now just because of something you said," Betty smiled reassuringly. Marie entered the house at Betty's beckoning and followed her into the living room.

"Please have a seat, Marie." Looking around the mid-sized room Marie saw what appeared to be a well-used, yet well-kept sofa. She sat down allowing its comfortable cushions to envelope her petite frame.

"The water in the teapot will boil soon and we can sit and talk awhile before you must leave. I have some exceptional tea you must try!" Betty's hospitality was second to none, but her hermit lifestyle did not contribute to many guests sharing stories with her. Marie knew she was lucky to even have this chance with Betty, but she also had an agenda she wanted to keep.

"No offense, Ms. Bekkett, but the forecast is calling for increasing rainfall. I was really hoping to get into the field and see what you told me about before the ground became too impassable," Marie hoped she sounded more patient than she felt.

"Deary, I know the weather as well as you. The fact is, I called off my boys. Told them to stay home and not venture out this way. I knew it would not be a good day for this quest. I would have called you as well, but I couldn't recall your number," Betty replied.

"Mam, I've set aside all my plans today for this very meeting. We discussed this months ago to make sure you and I had the entire day to allow me to see for myself this mystery site," Marie said trying hard not to sound insolent.

"Honey, I'm surprised you would want to position yourself so close to something you have feared for so long. Besides, it's only folklore. I don't even believe there's one iota of truth about it. But, given the weather, it makes no difference. You will not be going there today," Betty said in a manner to end the topic of discussion.

Hoping the weatherman was wrong, Marie decided to have some tea and chat with Ms. Bekkett. If the sun snuck from behind the clouds, she would have her chance to fulfill her plans for this day. "In that case, then, I'll have my tea with some sweetener."

"Oh, not this tea. It's perfectly brewed. You won't need to add any foreign substances to try and improve its flavor," Betty responded from the kitchen. Marie bit her tongue to keep quiet. She despised being told how she did or did not like something.

"So, Marie, I hear you came back to Bekkett after receiving a history degree. Why would you return after experiencing the freedoms of the city?" Betty asked.

"Truth is, this is all I know. The big city life wasn't for me. Besides, the history I love is all around us. Not many people have the chance to see forts where battles once waged. Where blood was shed for the ability to call a piece of land home. To search once blood-soaked fields for artifacts. It's not just a degree. It's my hobby. I love it here," *sort of*, Marie added in her head.

"Do tell me, dear. What do you know about the history of this ranch and the city that stole its name?" Betty inquired.

Marie was hesitant to get sidetracked, but she was stalling for the sun anyway. She also understood there were far too few people who found interest in history. Her fascination with it was often a topic that put others to sleep.

For forty-five minutes Marie brought to life the pages of history she rarely had the chance to discuss. In 1837, Pete Bekkett, along with his wife, son, and three daughters decided to move west. The crowds along the Virginia harbor were more than Pete enjoyed. Pete sold every possession he had, including his farrier business, and brought two of his employees with him. He knew if he were going to till the land he would need more than himself and his son.

Although his first decade in the dry and desolate landscape was difficult, by 1848 Pete had been as successful along the foothills of the Rocky Mountains as he had been in the bustle of his former life. Through bartering and kind heartedness, he forged friendships and partnerships with most people he encountered. His ranch became a well-known safe haven for gold seekers, hungry travelers, and friends.

Pete's son grew up, married, and had children of his own. It appeared Pete's success would continue for generations. Instead, in June of 1860, Pete went hunting and never returned. His son, Jerry, carried the bitterness of his father's departure with him. Jerry became consumed by disturbing ideas and was a recluse. He told strange stories when he was in town about a beast that killed his father. He was ostracized by those around him. Eventually he became an outcast, but not before a group of investors from Chicago traveled west.

In 1876, the Double K Ranch had grown so large, Jerry and his sons, Luke and Chad, were unable to work the 5,000-acre ranch on their own. A group of investors from Chicago were naïve to his negative reputation, and Jerry sold much of his land to the men who planned to develop an outpost for westward travelers. Jerry's one condition to selling his property was for the buyers to agree to name the newly formed town Bekkett in honor of Pete's beloved spirit.

"The Bekkett family has lived on the original 200 acres of the ranch from one generation to the next. You are here now because of that legacy." Marie concluded her story telling and waited for a response.

After an unfilled pause in conversation, Marie continued, "Of course, I believe there is more to Pete's disappearance than simply a bear or other *known* wild animal. Otherwise, I would not have contacted you, Ms. Bekkett. I hope my conspiracy theory about your family lineage isn't offensive."

"If I were offended by such theories, I would have vacated this region years ago. It is part of being a Bekkett. The mystery of our past is in our blood," Betty paused and looked at the drops of rain dripping down the window. "It's clear you enjoy your history. Sadly, your degree did not advance you in the full knowledge of the Bekkett family's past. You are only able to provide discourse of what every other historian around here has said. But remember dear, those historians only showed up to this region *after* it was settled. There are other stories that very few have ever heard. Some secrets have been sheltered from the world around us. I like you and I like your willingness to sit here and humor an old lady."

Marie raised her eyebrows and leaned forward. She was hoping her trip here today was not in vain.

"Sweetie, I want you to come back tomorrow. I have a few documents I need to dig up. When I find them, I think you are the rightful heir to possessing them." Betty suddenly stood and walked to the front door. "Thank you for your heartfelt interest in this community. When you return, please come alone." With those words, Betty opened the door and shooed Marie outside.

September 12, 2013 – 10:00PM

Gavin sat in front of the TV, bored. As usual, he sat alone in his apartment not willing to subject himself to the lame nightlife Bekkett had to offer. A few run-down bars in town catered to those with increasingly wrinkled skin. They were the patrons who seemed to think they owned a DeLorean whisking them back twenty years each time they crossed the threshold of the smoke swollen bars. He had spent too many nights inside those dens working on stories for the paper. He was not about to willingly subject himself to such misery. He also found it much less expensive to purchase his own Kentucky bourbon than to pay a bartender to do the same. Considering his options of a poorly lit, smoky bar compared to his lonely apartment, he chose the latter.

Staying home was also wise because he had promised Marie he would help her with her latest research project. She was cryptic with its nature, and it was beginning to upset him that she asked for help then refused to trust him with any information. What had she hoped to accomplish by keeping him in the dark? He had picked up his phone six times tonight to text her. Each time he typed, "I'm too busy to help," but guilt overwhelmed him, and he deleted the text. Deep down, or possibly right on the surface, he knew it was not guilt. He was curious. And Marie was cute.

Some girls in Bekkett did not age well. When you spend your life growing up with someone, you see their flaws – internal and external. Maybelline can only cover so much. But Marie was different. She entered the public school system when they were both in second grade. In a small town of familiar faces, she was the mysterious new girl. She was quirky and funny, and everyone seemed to like her. She was cute back then as well. Sadly, after her parent's disappearance and death, Marie withdrew. While beauty radiated from her olive skin, dark brown hair, svelte waistline, and green eyes, there was a discomforting pallor that encircled Marie.

It is why Gavin could hardly believe it when Marie first came to him two weeks ago. She reminded him more of elementary aged Marie than high school Marie. She was talking. A lot. She rambled on about historical landmarks which existed despite the secrecy of their location. She said it was Bekkett's "Ark of the Covenant."

Gavin closed his eyes and remembered their conversation.

"Gavin, my life mission… well, my mission for the last 10 years, has been to shed light on all the stories we hear in this town. There are so many mysterious tales, and I want to know what really happened."

"What are you talking about, Marie?" Gavin had asked while also looking at her like she was a bit crazy.

"Just trust me. There are weird things that have occurred since the late 1800's and I intend to find some proof!"

Gavin shook his head and let out a small laugh. "Marie, I think you're losing it."

Upon hearing his poorly thought-out words, Marie shook her index finger at Gavin and said, "Fine! I don't want your help." With that, she turned around and took a step toward the exit.

Recognizing the absurdity of pushing her away, he blurted out, "Wait! Is this about," he paused not wanting to say the words, then continued, "Ya know, the big scary monster?"

Marie paused and kept her hand on the doorknob and her back toward Gavin. He knew her exit was mere seconds away. "Listen, Marie. It doesn't matter what it's about."

Then she turned that beautiful olive skin face toward Gavin and looked slightly over her shoulder. A wisp of her mahogany brown hair brushed across her forehead, and her slender fingers came off the door and gently pushed the strands of hair away from her eyes. Those deep green eyes penetrated his soul. He knew if he did not help now, she may never speak with him again. So it was, out of a selfish desire to spend more time with Marie, Gavin said, "Tell me when you're ready, or not at all. Let me help you."

He hoped his agreement to her silly hunt for this mystery's answer would prompt her to tell him more. Instead, she turned away again and opened the door. She walked out and as the door began to slowly close behind her, he could hear her say, "Thanks. I'll let you know what I need later."

And, so, he became obsessed, not only with thoughts of walking hand in hand with Marie, but also with helping her solve this mystery. He could only assume she was looking into the famed Bekkett Beast. He had written articles and interviewed residents about it during his tenure at the paper. However, nothing ever came of his commentaries and investigative digging. He knew her search would end with disappointment as well. The tale of the beast was far more a joke than a realistic possibility.

Turning off the muted television, Gavin knew his thoughts of holding Marie's hand would never come to fruition if he did not actually get to work. The only clues he received about her hunt was when she asked him to help with some mapping. At first, he thought her request was so simple. He explained that a quick GIS search would probably suffice. Marie stared quizzically at Gavin, and he quickly realized her skills with a computer were far more along the academic nature of research than with satellite imagery.

Getting to work, it took Gavin only a few hours to log onto Rice County's GIS mapping system and pinpoint the property Marie had inquired about: The Double K Ranch. Per her request, he zoomed in as close as possible and saved a screen shot. Realizing he just captured the lamest of all maps, he took a more picturesque approach. For the next two hours, he printed the entire 200-acre ranch onto forty-seven separate 8x11 pieces of paper. He labeled each photo and stacked them so she could easily recreate the entire ranch from any sizable room. He was absurdly obsessed with gaining her favor. Yet, these forty-seven pages offered little guidance as to what he was searching for.

As he stared at the stack of papers, he realized he was no closer to helping her find answers. The printed maps were not going to guide him toward any meaningful answers. To be thorough and complete, given few instructions, Gavin also decided to print the layout of the ranch using a topographical map. He hoped the elevation differences may be of assistance. Aside from the creek and the house itself, which sat thirty feet lower than the nearby fields, most of the land was flat. As any large field should be. There was, however, one anomaly to the ranch, which was on the furthest southwest parcel. The topographical map showed a slight increase in elevation, almost imperceptible at first. In comparing it to the satellite photo, he could see no obvious difference in elevation.

The one-dimensional pages on his floor were never going to gain Marie's respect. Gavin knew the coming hours would hold a trip to the Double K Ranch. He looked at his watch stunned to see six hours had passed since he began this futile paper trail. He was now likely the sole person in this town to still be awake. It was four in the morning, and he was suddenly aware of his fatigue. He sauntered to the bedroom and flopped onto his bed. Gavin nodded off to thoughts of Marie hugging him for his discovery of . . . well, what he discovered he was not exactly sure of. But her hug, even though it was imaginary, reassured him he had stumbled upon something useful.

September 13, 2013 – 9:00AM

After a few hours of rest, the disruption to his sleep-filled silence nearly forced him off his bed. Sitting up, Gavin looked around the darkened room trying to decipher what startled him awake. The faint light glowing in his room was his first clue of what shook him from his slumber. He picked his cell phone off the top of the nightstand and squinted at the notification. The pretty hue of the screen betrayed the emergency warning that had illuminated his phone. The weather service had issued an alert for flash flooding.

As Gavin ran his hand through his short blonde hair, he laughed at the absurdity of the warning. *How could Sand Creek ever crest its fifteen-foot banks?* It was aptly named Sand Creek because its water-swollen depths, at the height of spring run-off, capped at about three feet. One was far more likely to enjoy the sandy bottom than water sports on the creek. Gavin pulled the cord to his cheap blinds, but they refused to obey his command to open. He finagled the cord side-to-side until the faux wood slats lifted away from the windowsill. The world outside was gray with bits of rain. Rain being too strong a word for the fleeting bits of moisture falling.

Gavin shrugged off the warning. He sauntered into the kitchen, still trying to fully awaken. He opened the cupboard above his coffee pot and pulled out a white number four coffee filter. He placed it into the top of his coveted coffee pot and filled the machine with fresh ground beans and a ridiculous amount of water. While Gavin waited for the coffee to brew, he went to the bathroom. After emptying his bladder, he washed his hands and face. Rather than go to the work of sculpting his hair, he grabbed a ball cap he picked up in Canada. He had recently visited a friend in Saskatoon, Saskatchewan, and obediently purchased a baseball cap from the berry farm they visited. It was Gavin's tradition to buy a hat at each locale he visited as a memory of the trip.

He dressed and rubbed on some deodorant in an attempt to keep the stench of not bathing at bay. He took a quick glance in the mirror with an approving grin. Gavin ventured back into the kitchen and chose a 20-ounce tumbler from his cupboard. He added a splash of half and half to the insulated coffee mug and poured a healthy cup of this life-giving liquid. He turned back toward his modest apartment and packed his travel bag with surveillance gear. The coffee traveled to his brain causing Gavin to recall the ridiculous maps he printed the night before. He shook his head in contempt and made a mental note to begin saving for a drone.

"Amateur," Gavin said to the empty walls of his white-washed apartment.

It took Gavin half an hour to get ready and gather equipment. He loaded his gear into his car and sat in the driver's seat before using the remote to open the garage door. Backing out of the warmth of his garage, he was stunned by the grey clouds spilling thunderous drops of rain. Just a half-hour earlier, the clouds were merely spitting fits of sporadic moisture. Now, the raindrops had increased in size and intensity and were assaulting his windshield with disdain. Gavin wondered if there was more to the flash flood warning than he first thought.

His drive to the road bordering Double K Ranch was uneventful. There was no obvious indication of rising water to fear besides a few deeper-than-usual puddles on the roadway which caused his car to rattle and shake as his tires sank into the voids the town carelessly failed to fill. As he drove on, Gavin curiously listened to the one AM station he could hear without an earful of static. It was the usual over-talkative, self-appreciating host he did not care to listen to. After enduring five minutes of the man's rant about the creativity of his own opinions, a weather update finally aired.

Gavin turned up the radio thankful for the interruption from the annoying DJ. He listened as the same warning from his morning text was re-iterated. Due to continuous rainfall in the mountains to the west, the creek beds were beginning to fill with water. Authorities promised to continue monitoring the situation. They also seemed to prematurely encourage residents downstream to seek higher ground. The weather report was appropriately timed. As their warnings to climb to safety were aired, Gavin crossed over Sand Creek on his final approach to Double K Ranch. Looking to his left, the banks appeared to be only a few inches higher than normal. He saw no increasing current or reason to climb a nearby tree.

"Stupid media," Gavin said only to himself. "Always full of non-existent drama in order to instigate fear." Gavin failed to recognize he, too, was a journalist and often hoped for exaggerated truths to create a story worth printing.

He crossed the bridge over the embellished depths of Sand Creek and searched for a place to stop. After a couple of hundred yards, he found a widened portion of the dirt road, pulled over, and parked. He pulled his Nikon from its padded case and set up the camera on the five pound, three-point tripod. He chuckled thinking about the redundancy of a manufacturer highlighting that their tripod had three points of contact. He shook his head when he realized he actually fell for the marketing scheme. Still, it was designed to sustain heavy winds and not budge.

Once Gavin was satisfied with the set-up of his equipment, he began taking panoramic photos of Double K Ranch and its outlying fields. Not wanting to trespass and explain that to his dad, a retired police officer, Gavin stood roadside and used the telephoto lens to take close-ups of the large field. In the extreme distance, he could see the elevated portion of the field that his topographical map from the night before had highlighted.

He had grown up around here and had never noticed it before. Of course, he had no need to see such a sight prior to now.

Gavin could not help but wonder if that elevated portion of land had anything to do with Marie's quest. He played with the 500-millimeter zoom lens to gain the right amount of focus. It added ten inches to the length of the camera but was worth the extra space it took. Zooming as close as he could to the target portion of land, Gavin peered at the camera's 3.5-inch screen. He swore he saw movement at the highest point of the field. He cleared moisture off the screen and looked again. Switching to the viewfinder of the camera for better focus, he watched for movement. There it was. Someone was coming up, appearing to rise out of the ground. He saw the person turn their back and then descend into the ground again. After five minutes, he saw the person ascend again into the open field. The person turned and faced him as if they knew he was watching. He jumped back from the camera's viewfinder startled and hoped he had not been discovered. It was clear who it was.

"Betty!?" Gavin exclaimed. "What are you doing out in the rain? In the ground?!" Gavin continued his monolog. Then Betty bent down, lifted a piece of wood or metal, and dropped it onto the surface of the field. Gavin realized she was closing the door to some sort of hatch. He was elated with this discovery. Once again, his mind wandered toward the thought of Marie hugging Gavin tightly when he told her what he had found.

Gavin was thrust back into reality when he noticed the downpour increased in intensity and his rain gear was beginning to meet its threshold. Gavin figured he had as much information as he could gather today and thought it best to pack it up and head home. He carefully removed the camera from the tripod and dried it off under the covering of his car. He placed it back into its padded case to preserve its precious data. He folded the tripod and set it on the backseat floorboard to let the water drip onto the floormats of his car.

September 13, 2013 – 2:30 PM

As Gavin drove back toward his apartment, his mind drifted to what Betty could have been doing underneath the field. What mystery was she concealing? Was Marie in jeopardy of diving headfirst into something too big for her to deal with alone? Did Betty have some secret group of slaves held captive in some dank dungeon? Too many questions and only a few answers led Gavin to the Town of Bekkett's joint museum and library. One thing this small town prided itself in was its bland history.

Gavin grew up around here and knew the boring tale of how Bekkett swelled to notoriety with the wealth of one lucky rancher. As the rancher grew wealthy, those unfortunate few who left the bustle of Chicago for what they were told was a better life, grew poorer. Those who had made the desolate trek west were ill-prepared to tackle the terrain of the mountains. Many hit the elevation of the first great hillside and turned back in fear. Of those who failed to trek over the mountainside, some moved south toward Denver. However, most settled in and around Bekkett as it was the closest haven of hope. Those slackers who failed to traverse the landscape used the proximity of Bekkett to the mountains to venture upward in search of gold on the weekends. The population increase from the failed westward travelers allowed Bekkett's population to surge to a modest town of 50,000 residents. But as the gold seekers died off, so did the desire to stick around. The town finally nestled down to 25,000 unlucky souls. And yet, despite his dissatisfaction with the town, Gavin never had the courage to leave everything he knew.

The museum-library seemed as old as the town itself. In fact, Gavin was quite sure it was one of the original structures, at least at its core. Throughout the years, the building had been renovated as necessary to prevent an undesirable collapse. The museum was on the second floor of the building with its rotating artifacts stored in the basement. The main floor housed the library where Gavin was now sitting. He had gone to the historical section of books and pulled a few from the shelf and began looking through them to see if he spotted anything of value.

September 13, 2013 – 3:10 PM

Marie debated about calling Gavin to clue him on what she was after. She liked him but was fearful this hunt for the Bekkett Beast would convince him she had lost her marbles. Instead, she decided to wait until she had more solid evidence, if she had more information, before she would divulge to him what it was she was seeking. She paced her apartment waiting to hear from Betty. Marie had given Betty her phone number yesterday when Betty said to come alone today. Five times already Marie had gone to her car, started the engine, and put it in reverse before deciding the last thing she could do was show up unannounced and erase Betty's kindness.

So, Marie paced. She sat down at her computer a few times to peruse her meticulous notes. She paced some more. She turned on her pathetic 19" TV to the one station that had reception using her rabbit ears antennae. It was the news. She hated the news. But they were droning on about the rain, so she mindlessly listened. When the flood warnings were announced, Marie perked up. She needed to get to the Double K Ranch before any truth of the rising water came to fruition.

Patience waiting on others was not one of Marie's strong points. She thought it slightly ironic she could sit in front of a computer screen researching projects for days at a time searching for mere sentences among volumes of documents. Yet when it came to waiting for another person, Marie lacked tolerance. At ten after three, Marie's cell phone chirped to life.

"Hello!" Marie nearly screamed into the receiver.

"Marie, its Ms. Bekkett. I wanted to let you know I have found the documents I informed you about when we spoke yesterday. However, I am afraid this rain is beginning to saturate the roads around my ranch. I fear you driving here today with the forecasts we are hearing."

"It's not a problem, mam. I had a very patient driving instructor. I can handle just about any condition," Marie said convincingly.

"Well, I'm not going to tell you no. After all, I did drench myself retrieving these documents. I'd like something good to come from my venture into the rainstorm. Something I haven't done since I was a young teenager." Marie did not catch the meaning behind this statement at first. It wasn't until she assured Betty she was on her way right now that it registered what she had said. *Was she telling me she had not been in a rainstorm for 60 years? Or did she simply mean it has not rained this hard in that time frame?*

With Marie's knowledge of what she was seeking and what secrets Betty may hold, it was easy to assume Betty truly had not stepped foot outside during a hard rain. If stories had been passed down in her family, it would be assumed a sure suicide to be drenched, in an open field, with nowhere to hide, while the moisture fell from the sky. That was the beast's feeding ground.

Marie rushed to her Ford Focus and hurried toward Double K Ranch. Turning onto the usually dry, dusty back roads felt like a new world in this storm. There were dark puddles of brown water littering the surface. Evidence of a street that was not maintained very often. The shoulders of the road were soft and beginning to drop off the side in places. Marie stayed in the center of the lane knowing she would not meet many cars in which to play chicken.

Arriving at the Double K Ranch brought a greater sense of relief than Marie realized she was holding on to. Her fingers were a bit tight from gripping the steering wheel. Her eyes were tired from the sheer focus of watching the roadway through a rain spattered windshield. Betty must have been waiting for Marie's arrival. The front door swung open the moment Marie set foot on the covered front porch. Betty had a steaming cup of tea in her grip and with a smile immediately served it to Marie.

"Please, sip some tea and warm your body. You don't want to get too cold out there in this weather. The rain alone is curse enough."

"Thank you, Ms. Bekkett. Again, your hospitality is second to none." Marie removed her muddy shoes and left them by the front door. She could not risk upsetting Betty by tracking mud through the house. Although, in reality, Marie knew Betty had her share of muddy feet traipsing through these halls. One more set now may not even faze her.

Betty directed Marie into the kitchen where they both sat at the eloquently hand carved table. "This is a beautiful piece of furniture, Ms. Bekkett. Was it made by one of your relatives?"

"Please, Marie, I'm Betty. And, thank you. My late husband, Mike, made this table with his father when Mike was only about eight years old. It has been in our family since I moved onto the ranch in 1958. We were married when I was in my late teens. Mike's parents were more than happy to move off the ranch and into more suitable living quarters in town. They sold the ranch to us for mere pennies, and I have lived here ever since. Mike loved this table and had many fond memories of family gatherings for as long as he can remember."

"It seems you are a very blessed woman, Betty."

"Well, blessings ebb and flow, my dear. I know I have few years left on this beautiful earth before my Maker brings me to my rightful home. And they are lonely years. Although you may not have guessed it, my two sons and my daughter want nothing to do with me. I have wept all I can for the loss of not knowing my children and grandchildren. I would say the tears I've shed may now be coming back to haunt us all with this storm we're experiencing. Maybe it's just the continued curse of the Bekkett's."

Betty's words trailed off and she was clearly thinking of a time and place other than this kitchen. The sound of the rainfall was now evidently clear as Marie let the silence envelope the two of them. After what seemed a full five minutes, Betty came to life again.

"I will outwit them, you know," Betty said with a sly smile.

"I'm sorry, who?" Marie asked.

"My kids. They left Bekkett and the responsibilities of Double K Ranch behind to flee from the family history. Some Bekketts loved the tales, others feared them. My children loathed the stories and wanted no part in the continuance of tradition."

"So, how did you outwit them?"

"My will is set and sealed. Each of them must come home, to the Double K, if they want any part of the family fortune. In my departing, they will be forced to face their fears and insecurities. And they will only discover then that the secrets of the ranch are now in your hands. They waived their rights to successorship when they waved goodbye. The money they can have. The legend they cannot."

Marie could not help but smile. There was much more to Betty than met the eye. Marie wished she had more time to sit and chat. But, for now, time was not a luxury. The storm continued to spit out reminders that time was of the essence. Marie was anxious to get the documents she came for and to leave for higher ground as soon as possible.

"You know, Betty, I really do want to urge you to consider leaving the ranch tonight. The weather forecasts continue to warn of rising waters. I fear it's not safe for you to stay here. Especially by yourself."

"I'm not leaving. This is my home. I have no friends in town and nowhere else to go. And I will *not* stay at one of those cheap hotels in town!"

As if on cue, the phone rang. Betty answered it, listened for a moment, and then chuckled as she placed the receiver back on the base. "I half wonder if you didn't plan that call. It was the sheriff's department. Some recording about mandatory evacuations. If they want me gone, they can come get me. But

I'm not leaving without a fight. No sense in you or the sheriff trying to convince me otherwise."

Turning from the phone, Betty reached into a satchel on the counter and pulled out several brown leather-bound journals. Marie eyed the journals and knew right away these were not recently obtained. They were worn, yet well maintained. Her best estimate was that they were at least 100 years old. Maybe more. It would take much patience and care to look at each page. This was the kind of patience she enjoyed.

Betty broke the silence, "These are the documents I want you to have." With that, she slid them toward Marie. "They are the Bekkett family heirloom. Only a Bekkett by blood has ever seen these journals. You are the rightful heir for the stories they contain."

Marie opened the cover of the top journal, but Betty promptly closed it. "I would love for you to remain with me and devour the words contained in these journals. Truth be told, I'd love just to see your reaction. However, this weather isn't improving. The sheriff's department has deemed this area off limits. I may be willing to risk my youthful life, but I will not allow you to risk yours. You must now leave." Just like yesterday, Betty abruptly stood, walked to the front door, and indicated with her hands it was time for Marie to leave. Without hesitation or argument, Marie slipped on her shoes, looked outside, and paused. She had secured the journals inside the satchel Betty provided and clung tightly to the secrets she had longed to know.

"Betty. I sense I may not see you again. I don't mean to scare you," Marie paused, "but I do believe trouble is on the horizon. Maybe it's because you've piqued my interest with hidden stories. Maybe it's just the rising water. I only wish we had met years earlier and time was not now our enemy. If I don't see you on this side of heaven, I hope to be greeted by you at the Pearly Gates. Thank you is merely too short, a phrase, to describe my gratitude." With tears swelling in her eyes, Marie took a page out of Betty's play book and suddenly turned and walked away.

September 13, 2013 – 5:00 PM

Two hours into his search, Gavin was beginning to see cross-eyed. He was blown away by the sheer volume of books, journals, and newspaper clippings that had been amazingly well preserved.

When Gavin was younger, his dad would share vague details of cases he was working. He would quiz Gavin on what to look for, how to interpret statements, and when to make the arrest. Using those investigative skills, and his talent to comb through fine details with acuity, he narrowed his search. He focused only on information surrounding the land adjacent to the present-day Double K Ranch. He did not want to narrowly concentrate on only one plot of land, as in its hay-day, Double K was sprawling.

Oddly enough the archives had mounds of documents about much of Bekkett's origins, except for about 10 years of information that was nearly missing. There were scraps of news here and there, but for the most part, a decade of Bekkett's history was thrown to the winds of time. These gaps nudged his curiosity, and he dug deeper.

He set book after book aside, quickly flipping through the pages in search of relevant data. Gavin tossed aside a weathered, brown journal and as it gently landed on the discarded pile of books and notes, he rubbed his thumb and middle finger together. This book had a different texture. It did not have the old, dry texture like so many of the other leather covers he had been touching. This one had a supple touch. It felt as though he had just picked it up from the store. He knew leather could retain the oils from one's skin which meant this book had been held. Often.

Gavin stopped his shuffling and picked the journal from the top of the pile he had callously tossed it onto. He gently flipped through the pages looking for something to catch his eye. No words or pictures jumped out at him, and no pages fell open to indicate definitive creases in the spine of the binding. He would have to be more meticulous with his search.

On his third search of the journal, he realized there was a folded page. The crease was set as the passage of time pressed it into resembling a single page. The line of the crease was barely visible. Carefully, Gavin tugged at the edge of the page to reveal what had been folded within. His first reaction was a chuckle. He saw a drawing akin to nothing more than a third-grade student would create. If it were not for the condition of the journal cover, he may have moved on and given this sketch no more attention. He knew there had to be more to it than a laughable picture. Under the drawing were scribbled notes, piquing his curiosity. He squinted and brought the page closer to his face for clarity. The penmanship was poor, at best, and he could not make out more than a bit of gibberish. But the gibberish was clear enough: "This ate my horse." The caption was underneath the drawing and Gavin realized "this" was referring to the picture above.

Gavin examined the drawing and recognized it as a near spitting image of the Tasmanian Devil from his days growing up watching cartoons. Except this beast had no comical value and was truly a horrific sight. The hair overtook most features, yet it was clear this image was of something possessing more than four limbs. At the end of the upper appendages, were claws with very distinct points. The mouth was gaping open, with a dark abyss absorbing its throat. If it were not a black and white drawing, Gavin was sure there would be swaths of red around the open mouth.

Knowing he was not permitted to subject the pages to a photo copier, Gavin silently removed his phone from his pocket and took several pictures. He carefully folded the page along the crease he had found and set the page flat against the others. Closing the journal, he meticulously put it back in the buried mound of papers.

As Gavin left the library it was obvious this is what Marie had hired him to investigate. He could not fathom what, specifically, she was seeking, but he was intrigued more than any other story he had covered for this town. Gaining insight into what Marie was after, he could barely contain his excitement at the caption and drawing he had just discovered. Driving home, he flipped on the radio only to hear alert tones again. The flash flood warning had been extended through tomorrow and people were advised to stay away from low lying ground near waterways. Gavin smiled at the ridiculous thought of rain soaking the ground to that extent. He lived here his entire life and had seen plenty of torrential downpours. None had produced the flooding being predicted. Society was becoming more and more concerned about lawsuits, and he was convinced the rambling reports were to protect themselves from pecuniary blame.

***

As Marie navigated the rain soaked back roads, she cursed herself for her parting words to Betty, *"I sense I may not see you again."* What had she been thinking? Did Betty put something in her tea? Why was she so doom-and-gloom all of a sudden? She could not shake how pathetic she must have sounded. Marie picked up her phone to call Betty. There was no way she wanted those words to be her farewell.

Marie glanced at her phone to get to the keypad. It was then she noticed a text from Gavin. She swiped at her phone's main screen to open the text. "I found a unique pic. Call me ASAP." Marie activated the voice texting system and responded. "Leaving Double K now. Home in twenty." She hit send and waited for the signal to show the message had taken its proper course. Then, curious when Gavin sent the text, she scrutinized the screen more closely. Too closely.

September 13, 2013 – 6:00 PM

The jarring of the car was violent. Marie lost grip of the wheel momentarily, as it pulled hard right. Her phone slipped from her hand, and she heard it thud against the floorboard. She clutched the steering wheel while simultaneously looking up and out the windshield. Somehow the car swerved too far toward the right and she was in the soft shoulder. The wheel shimmied left and right and left and right over and over as the tires bounced along the ruts of the dirt. Her fingers tightened around the steering wheel as if her petite grip would assuage the car. The momentum of her 2000-pound Focus was more than she could control. Mashing the brake pedal, she hoped to stop this nightmare, but it was too late. The car dropped off the slope of the road and down into a once empty drainage ditch.

The passenger side of the car flipped sideways and quickly met the rain-soaked ground. Glass shattered from every window of the car. Marie shut her eyes as if protecting her vision from broken glass was the primary goal. The car lurched forward, then came to a sudden stop, resting on its side. Sir Isaac Newton's Law of Gravity took on a jarringly new reality as Marie was thrown from her 90-degree sitting position. She hung suspended in the air, only to be held by man's made genius – the seat belt. But that genius also had a downfall. The force of the crash caused its pretensioner to hold her in place. There was no moving the seatbelt to unfasten it. She had no immediate choice but to be suspended as if on some cheap carnival ride.

***

Gavin was beginning to worry. It had been a full 45 minutes since he received Marie's text stating she was on her way home. He knew the drive. Even if she had taken the long route to her apartment, she would still have arrived by now. The moment he received her text, he drove to her place. He was there within five minutes but knocked on the door anyway just in case there had been a delay in sending the text. Somehow, beyond Gavin's grasp of understanding, cellular waves were swallowed between towers despite the flat terrain surrounding the region. Whether it was a bird's errant flight path, sunbursts, or a ghoulish atmospheric interference, Gavin could not say. But he experienced the loss of texts more times than he could recall. After Marie did not answer the door, he impatiently waited in his car. He watched the clock, peered at the rain, mindlessly listened to music, and still time would not speed up.

After 30 minutes, he sent her a brief text. "At ur place waiting to meet u." Afraid it sounded too much like a date, he added, "With vital info."

Allowing ten more minutes to pass with no response, worry began to set in. Gavin was sure something had happened to Marie. It was growing even darker than usual with the gray clouds holding the sun ray's captive far above. Gavin considered his options and chose to drive the most logical route to the Double K Ranch. If Marie was not there, at least then he could hope she stopped at the store, or salon, or somewhere safe. He tried soothing his thoughts by telling himself she had not checked her phone and did not know he had been waiting for her at her apartment.

***

Marie awoke, not realizing she had been unconscious. She was unsure when her head had clouded causing her to pass out. Sadly, her throbbing head screamed she was now awake.

Confusion encompassed her as her limp body continued to succumb to gravity's pull. Blood rushed to her hanging extremities and her hair reached helplessly for the ground. Her head was pounding, and the right side of her body was going numb from the pressure of her body cutting into the seatbelt.

Her phone's distinct text tones brought her back to reality. With no idea where the phone was, she focused on releasing herself from this position. Looking to her left, she saw a shard of glass protruding from the window. She pulled it from its temporary home and checked the edge. The tempered glass had done its job well and shattered into pieces. The larger piece she grabbed also broke into smaller pieces rendering it unable to be used as a cutting device.

It was getting darker outside causing fear to settle in. Only Gavin knew where she had been, and even that only by text. She could not be sure he even checked his phone recently. Marie was going to be her only rescuer. Moving against the pull of the world, Marie twisted her body and reached upward. Every abdominal muscle screamed in protest. Setting aside their cries of detest she was able to reach outside the open driver's window. Grabbing onto the roof of her car, she pulled herself up just slightly. It was enough to allow her to wiggle her legs up and to her left, finally freeing herself from the seatbelt's grip. She swung her legs over the center console and began to straighten them. The moisture on the exterior of the Ford was not ideal for a sure grip. Marie's hold slipped prior to extending her legs and she fell two feet into the now smashed passenger window.

It was not a graceful fall. Her head slammed into the interior light mounted on the ceiling and her elbow smashed into the pillar of the passenger side of the car as she crumpled to the ground. The shards of glass did not pierce her skin, but the pressure of a hundred sharp objects clawed at her arms and legs. Scraping the glass from her arm, Marie realized she was sitting in three inches of water. The ditch along the roadway had done its due diligence and was collecting water where her vehicle now protruded from. Becoming unnerved at the prospect of getting stuck in the cold, wet nether regions, she knew yelling would have no effect. Instead, she reached up and began honking her car horn.

After a few futile minutes, she gave up. She had to find her phone. The shadows in the car made searching for a dark object in a dark area much too difficult. By the grace of God, her phone began to ring! She paused long enough to orient herself with the ringing's location. It was behind her. She maneuvered around to look in the back seat just as she knew the phone would stop sending out its locating beacon. Long ago, she had set up her phone's flashlight to blink when she received texts and calls. Many taunted her for the annoyance of its strobe. She knew at this moment they would all be cursing themselves for not activating this little-used feature. The flashing of the light directed her attention to a puddle of water. She was grateful for purchasing the gargantuan protective phone case that would most likely survive a nuclear holocaust. Reaching for her phone, she picked it up out of the water and slid the green bar to the side.

"Hello!" It was a panicked scream. "Hello!" she repeated a second time. The phone did not answer. She pulled the phone away from her face and looked at the screen. 'Call Failed' taunted her.

Quickly pushing the call back button, she waited for the familiar ringing sound in the earpiece. A voice answered, but was cutting in and out, "He..o," was all she heard. Not knowing who it even was, she said as calmly as possible, "I'm in a ditch along the main route to Double K Ranch. My car is filling with water. Hurry."

Marie waited for a response, but again only heard bits and pieces of a male's voice. She repeated her cry for help into the phone and hoped enough words came through to piece together her message. She silently prayed it was not a solicitor who would only care for a sale or a scam, not interested in saving a life. When her spotty cellular service dropped the call again, she cursed under her breath for allowing her car to get the better of her and plunging into this hellish reality. She knew better than to fight the mechanics of a car. *I should have stayed at Betty's house for the night,* Marie thought. The realization of why she was on this lonely road turned her attention to the purpose of her journey: The secrets contained in the journals.

Using the flashlight on her phone, Marie frantically looked for the satchel containing the delicate century old books. She had not examined them when Betty entrusted them to Marie, but with one delicate touch she knew there was a rich history those books held secret. Straining her eyes, hope deflated, as she realized the satchel was missing. *It must have flown out of the car when I crashed!* Panic swept over Marie realizing how much trust Betty had put into Marie's hands. Along with her lost trust was the lost mystery that had been in her grasp just an hour before.

With a new sense of desperation, Marie was determined to free herself from her water tomb. She reached up with both hands and began jumping off the sloppy ground. After four attempts, she was able to get a grip on the edge of the car. She pulled herself up while at the same time kicking her feet to find any leverage to push her upper torso out the window. Once halfway out of the car, Marie swiveled her arms and pushed up against the car. She swung her legs out of the window and onto the driver side A-Frame, where she was able to perch herself and rest. She looked in front and toward the rear of her car scanning the waterlogged ditch for any signs of the treasure Betty had just given her. No satchel. No journals. Marie turned her attention to the murky roadway that had just spit her into this unforgiving gully.

She knew sitting on her car would not help her find the journals. Marie also feared any sudden movements might cause the Focus to shift and roll more. She would have to carefully traject herself off the car and onto the embankment. As she stood, her head rose above the surface of the roadway, but it was still two feet in front of her. With a verbal count to three, she thrust herself toward the road, landing with a thud. Her knees were slightly bent as she landed, and she slowly rose to a standing position. She stretched her arms and legs shaking the pain away. Glancing at her car, she both gasped and whimpered at her loss.

She scanned the roadway and saw nothing, although little could be seen along the blackened horizon. Heading towards Betty's house, Marie kept her head down hoping to locate any sign of the satchel or its contents. After an unproductive search, Marie assumed the satchel had followed her impetus into the ditch. She returned to her car deciding to descend back into the void she had just escaped. Sliding down the sloped edge of the roadway, she journeyed into the ditch, first walking in front of her car. The momentum prior to the crash would have kept the satchel moving forward. From the hood of her car, she slowly began traversing forward in the water reaching down every couple of feet and searching with her hands for her bag.

After one-hundred yards of her hopeless hunt, Marie climbed out of the ditch and into the adjacent wooded field. Her steps were slow and deliberate to prevent her adrenaline from pushing her too fast. Her head was on a swivel, turning left, then right, left, then right again. Thinking she saw the bag out of the corner of her eye, she periodically turned her head sharply, peering over one shoulder or the other. When she reached the distance she knew would be too far for the journals to have traveled, she headed back to her car. When she reached the front bumper, she turned to her left two steps, and walked toward the rear bumper. She walked in a straight line, one hundred yards ahead. Without success, she began a methodical search back and forth until she was at least sixty yards from the roadway. There was no possible way the satchel flew that far. She repeated the same path back to the rear of the vehicle and still could not find the satchel. It was too dark to continue her search and she feared the bag was irrevocably stuck underneath the weight of her car.

With her adrenaline draining, she became acutely aware of just how cold and wet she was. The trees lining the road had provided some shelter from the rain, but not enough to stay dry. Marie chided herself for not prioritizing her own rescue over that of the journals. Yet, her life mission had only moments before been in her grasp with the writings Betty had entrusted to Marie. How could she carry on knowing she had lost, and most likely destroyed, the answers she had desperately sought. Marie screamed into the night air. Should she walk back toward Double K Ranch and confess to Betty what had happened, get dry, and drink some hot tea? Or should she wait for whoever had called and was no doubt on the hunt to find her? Marie clambered back up to the roadway and pondered whether to go left or right. Double K Ranch was to her left. The town of Bekkett was to her right.

When Marie was young and faced with making a decision, she would chant eenie-meenie-miney-moe in her head. Just as she began to hum the tune, she realized the storm had let up slightly, quieting the constant sound of pattering rain. She turned her head, imperceptibly, aligning her ears with a familiar noise. She paused, held her breath, and focused. In the distance, nearly inaudible was the sound of a vehicle approaching. It was far off because she immediately scanned the distance of the roadway and could not see any headlights. She waited. The engine noise was coming from the direction of town. Without thinking, Marie turned right and ran. As soon as lights appeared on the horizon, she began frantically waving her arms. Those two tiny headlights looked like the eyes of her savior!

Marie slowed to a walk and put her hands down. The car slowed and came to a stop about ten feet in front of her. The headlights blinded her from seeing into the vehicle, but she heard the door open, and then footsteps running toward her. As the figure's shadow stepped in front of the headlights, her vision adapted, and she immediately recognized Gavin. Upon realizing who it was Marie ran toward him and they met in an embrace. It was not romantic in nature, simply one of pure relief at the sight of the other. Gavin pulled away first, saw Marie's drenched clothing and immediately removed his coat and wrapped it around her. He then instinctively grabbed her arm gently and escorted her to his car. He opened the front passenger door and she sat down with such relief. She immediately scanned the dash, turned the heat to high and directed the vents to blow on her torso.

Gavin sat in the driver's seat and turned to face Marie. "What happened? Are you okay? Where's your car? Is the road flooded over? Are you okay? What happened?" He couldn't stop repeating himself with curious questions.

"I'm fine. Don't worry about me. I don't care about my car. But we have to find the journals. They must have flown out of my car when it rolled. Drive ahead about a quarter mile. We *have* to find the journals!"

"Marie, no offense, but you're not thinking clearly. You're wet. You're cold. Apparently, you just survived a crazy car accident. You may have internal injuries. I don't know. But I do know the water *is* rising around here and we need to get back into town. Now." With that, Gavin put the car in reverse.

Marie opened her door and started to get out just as Gavin started moving. "What are you doing?! Get in the car and close the door!" Gavin yelled.

"I need to find the journals."

"You're crazy. This whole mystery is crazy. I'll help because I have some questions of my own, and because I wouldn't sleep well knowing I let you freeze out here alone tonight. Close your door." With that, Gavin switched into drive and slowly inched forward. He turned the lights to bright and they drove at a snail's pace looking for any signs of the journals.

"What exactly are we looking for?" Gavin asked.

"Betty gave me some valuable journals. I put them in a black and green satchel." Marie answered.

As they paralleled Marie's turned over car the headlights of Gavin's vehicle shined on the taillight of hers. "Is that it over there?" Gavin asked as he pointed to the reflective sheen.

"No. That's my car."

"What? You rolled your car into the ditch? I thought you got stuck in a pothole or something," Gavin gasped as he realized he was looking at the driver's side of her car. "You have to see a doctor. That had to have hurt more than you're willing to admit."

"Later," Marie muttered. "Right now, I need those journals."

Gavin's car rolled forward gaining imperceptible speed on the slight decline in the roadway. Marie pointed ahead and yelled, "Right there! Stop! Stop!"

Not wanting to incur the wrath of Marie, Gavin smashed his foot on the brake jolting both their heads toward the dash. "Sheesh! You scared the crap out of me, Marie! I see it."

Marie jumped out of the car, and ran toward the satchel relieved at its sight. She bent down and excitedly picked the satchel off the soaked roadway. Assuming the satchel did the job it was created for, document protection, she hadn't thought about making sure it was still shut tight. The zipper had slipped open a bit and as she pulled it up, gravity did its job. The journals fell out. "No!" Marie screamed. One of the journals landed on its back cover, allowing for a bit of protection from the moisture. The other blew open, releasing several loose pages into the wind.

"Hurry! Don't let those blow away!" Marie turned and hollered at Gavin. She pointed at the pages being tossed in the wind while wishing she had the power to stop the pages where they were.

Gavin took off after the pages as they began to blow down the road. Marie turned her attention to putting the remaining journals back into the satchel. Peering inside, she saw two more journals had not been wrested from the protection of the satchel. The journals she recovered were wet and she feared their secrets may forever be ruined. Running back to Gavin's car, she held the satchel inside the cover of the vehicle, while she stood outside waiting for Gavin. She grabbed one of the journals by the binding, turned the pages toward the floorboard, and lightly shook it. The pages of the journal huddled together clinging to one another for collective warmth.

How could I have been so careless? Betty entrusted these to me and not ten minutes later, I lost them in the worst storm of the century! Marie scolded herself silently.

Her self-blame was interrupted by Gavin's approaching footsteps. She looked up and he was holding his hand under his nearly soaked shirt. He was clearly trying to keep whatever he was holding from getting soaked even more. "I found three pages. I think that's all there was. Let's get in the car and get these on the dashboard so the heat can dry them up."

Marie sat in the car feeling completely defeated. She turned and looked at Gavin. She hoped the rain on her face would mask the tears swelling in her eyes. "Thank you." She wanted to say more. She wanted to tell him how utterly stupid she was feeling right now. But her guard was up and she wasn't about to let him know the shame she was feeling at this moment. Still, she was more than grateful he had come to her rescue.

They sat in silence for the first five minutes of the ride back into town. Gavin was the first to break the droning of the rain and the swishing of the windshield wipers. "Shouldn't you call the sheriff's department and let them know you were in an accident? In fact, I'm pretty sure you're required to call them." Gavin wanted to sound authoritative, but not overbearing.

"You're right, I probably should," agreed Marie. "But I'll wait till we're back home. I don't want them to tell me to wait here. I am freezing and need a change of clothes. Take me to my apartment. Please."

The rest of the ride home was equally as quiet as the first five minutes. Gavin had a thousand questions, but none seemed appropriate. He would wait until she was cleaned up and they could concentrate on what they both had discovered.

They pulled into her parking lot and Gavin turned to look at Marie before she went inside. "You have some explaining to do, Marie. You want my help, so I need you to open up a bit and clue me in on what you are after."

"You're right. It only seems fair that I fill you in."

"Good. I'm glad we agree. Go on in and get cleaned up. I'll run back to my place and gather up some documents I left there. I'll be back here in an hour, and you can give me the scoop then. Sound good?"

"Perfect. See ya then."

September 13, 2013 – 7:30 PM

Gavin had a short drive to his apartment. Of course, in Bekkett, most drives from one side of town to the other did not take all that long, especially at night when minimal traffic kept the roads mostly empty. The rain had not let up and the emergency alerts continued to chirp his phone to life. It was going to be a long night for first responders if the waters rose as projected. Gavin was finally beginning to believe the forecasts of the last twelve hours.

Gavin pulled into the parking lot of his apartment complex and was grateful for his upgraded apartment with attached garage. He pulled into the enclosure and the quietness settled in. He let out a slow, long breath, only then realizing how worried he had been. He stepped out of the car and walked into his main room squinting at the number of lights he had left on.

Gavin began to gather his mapping system, photos, and notes from his time at the library. While putting his research in order, he called his friend who was a deputy at the sheriff's department. Corey picked up his personal cell phone on the third ring.

"Hello, Gavin," Corey said flatly into the receiver. "Make it quick. I'm busy."

"What? Are you working?"

"Yep."

"Why? Did you transfer out of that cushy desk job of yours?"

"Heck, no, Gavin. But it's all hands-on deck. Command staff has mandated all personnel to work twelve hour shifts until the storm blows over. Great plan, too. I'm on hour fourteen!"

"Is it that bad? I saw the creek not that long ago and it hadn't risen more than a foot or two."

"Gavin, part of my job is to reduce the risk to the public. No, it's not that bad… yet. But there are fears it will continue to get worse. We are pre-evacuating homes all along the river, closing roads, and trying to stay ahead of this storm. What do ya need?

"Well, you remember Marie?"

"Yeah."

"She was out and about in the storm and her car flipped into a ditch. She got out and is fine. I am just curious if it needs to be reported?"

"Technically, yes. Where was it?"

"Next to the Double K Ranch. Well, near it, I guess. I'm not sure how close or not, really."

There was a pause on the other end of the line and Gavin wondered if he lost the call. Just as he was about to prod Corey for an answer, he heard Corey speak up. "I just checked our latest updates. That portion of road was officially closed about an hour ago. Not that anyone is out there to deter traffic, it is just one of the places we made a mandatory evacuation call. Once we are able, we will probably set up some barriers or road closed signs. All that to say we will not respond to any non-injury accidents. It's too dangerous. She can report it online. I'll make a quick note on our system."

"Thanks, Corey. I appreciate it. Stay safe out there."

"Will do. See ya, Gav."

September 13, 2013 – 8:30 PM

Gavin gave Marie an hour to get cleaned up then returned to her apartment. He put the car in park, removed his seat belt, reached into the front passenger seat, grabbed the backpack containing all his documents, and ran toward Marie's door. He knocked feverishly when he realized she had no awning to defend himself from the weather. He waited then moved the backpack into the front of his now unzipped jacket. He wanted to avoid the water penetrating through the mesh pack's material.

Gavin reached up to knock again just as Marie opened the door, stepped aside, and gestured for him to come inside. "You should've called. I would have unlocked the door and told you to just come on in," Marie told him.

"I'll keep that in mind for future tromps through the rain."

As Gavin doffed his coat and set the backpack down, he told Marie about his conversation with the sheriff's department, knowing she would be relieved at the lack of a request to return to the scene of the accident. What Gavin did not know was Marie was also silently glad she was not going to have to explain to the police she crashed because she was texting. She already felt enough shame of her own doing.

"I brewed some coffee. I thought we might have a long night ahead of us between your discovery and whatever those pages hold," Marie said as she pointed toward the journals. "If I haven't completely ruined them," Marie added under her breath.

Oblivious to her mumbling, Gavin replied, "Thanks. The stronger the coffee the better." He was already at work trying to connect his phone to her wireless network so he could print the page he captured while at the library. "Hey, do you know your network password? I'm trying to use your printer. I want to show you some of what I've come up with so far."

"Yes, I know my password. Give me your phone. I'll type it in for you." Marie trusted Gavin. She just did not want him to know her password was BekkettBeast. It would just add fuel to his fire that her obsession was a bit on this side of crazy. Not that he had ever said it, but she felt he was thinking it. Tonight, was the first time he actually showed any interest in her case other than his own desire to be close to Marie. Which is why she had tolerated him this far. She, too, was glad he had stuck around to help. They knew each other for years and she was happy to have a friend helping her cause.

Her parents would have been accepting of her research and drive. Since their disappearance, Marie had never felt close enough to others to trust with this passion of hers. She was scared this trek would be one she accomplished on her own. She needed support and validation on this journey and Gavin was the guy she wanted by her side in making this discovery. They had a connection of lost parents, whether due to death or desertion.

After typing in the password and verifying his phone picked up her wi-fi signal, she handed the device back to Gavin. "You should be good to go now. I got hooked up to the town's gigabyte data plan. Even this storm won't delay the delivery of data. Wow. Try saying that three times fast!" Marie added realizing she was beginning to sound like a commercial for internet speeds.

"Thanks, Marie. I'd hate to have a delay in the delivery of my data," Gavin taunted with a smile.

"I've laid the journal pages you were able to save from blowing away on the kitchen counter, on drying racks. I think it's too late to save whatever may have been on those pages, though. They're not legible at all. The journals are also a bit wet and I'm heartbroken to think I may have ruined the first real lead I've had since I began this quest years ago." Marie was shaking her head in disgust.

"Marie, you're being too hard on yourself. You are lucky to be alive. The pages would mean nothing if you had died in that car wreck." Gavin felt his soothing was not helpful, based on how big an arc Marie's eyes took as she rolled them.

To try and console her enough to move on Gavin added, "Let's work to see what we do have. It may be more than you anticipated. Besides, you have *a lot* of explaining to do. The journals will have plenty of time to dry while you tell me what, *exactly*, it is you are searching for. Why did you seek my help, anyways? I've had a bazillion questions but have kept my mouth shut. It's time to buck up, or I will leave you on your own."

Gavin knew that was not true, so he quickly added an incentive to keep himself around. "Besides, I found something today that may be connected, and I won't share unless you do first." Gavin wished he had stopped talking about twenty seconds sooner. He was starting to feel like a junior high adolescent with his I'll-show-you-mine-if-you-show-me-yours attitude.

Marie gave no indication of responding to him and Gavin found himself scrambling with words trying to get information without sounding rude. So, he rambled on. "The fact is Marie, you've failed to say a whole lot to me up to this point. I've humored you because I like y… to help you. But it's time you tell me, *specifically*, what you're looking to find in these pages. I'm done helping if you don't start talking."

Marie stood, turned away from Gavin, and walked into the kitchen. Gavin waited a moment then stood up and walked to the front door. "I was really hoping you'd be able to trust me more, Marie. I guess I'll see you around." With that, Gavin put his hand on the doorknob and began to turn it.

"Wait! I was just refilling your coffee! Sheesh. Sit down and prepare to think I'm a crazy loon," Marie quipped.

"That already crossed my mind when I saw your car, Marie."

Gavin turned away from the front door and walked toward Marie. He took the coffee mug from her hand and sat on the sofa. He was pretty sure he would have liked a nice cold beer for the story he was about to hear. But coffee would have to suffice. For the next hour, Marie filled Gavin in on all her knowledge, suspicions, stories, and half-known truths. Throughout her years in Bekkett, she had befriended many residents whose roots were firmly planted in this region. Many people would tell her tales passed down from one generation to the next. The common theme always revolved around a voracious scream that pierced the night air during storms. Those folks were eager to share their stories, but also ready to brush aside any truth. Most were sure it was legend and folklore only.

Marie spoke with such passion and conviction. She was desperate to finally discover definitive facts. Gavin could not help but find himself lost in the beauty of her story. And the ridiculousness of it. Even though Marie was convinced it was all real, Gavin was not yet ready to go all in. He listened but silently vowed he would be by Marie's side when they finally discovered it was a hoax. Gavin had grown up hearing similar stories. He assumed the stories were invented to bring new travelers to the area. It was nothing more than a clever tale to get desperate gold seekers to stop in Bekkett before they continued west. What a great ploy to spread the word in an age when social media was not available to help so efficiently. But tonight Gavin sat silently and listened to Marie.

September 14, 2013 – 1:00 AM

The rain intensified and, in the darkness, Sand Creek was quickly becoming a river like Bekkett had never seen before. The meager current was beginning to rival the most adventurous white-water river. Trees along the banks were beginning to lose ground and several of the less rooted ones already succumbed to the persuasion of the rising water, swept downstream, and snarled in a nest of other fallen vegetation and debris.

Where the banks of the creek were lower in elevation, the water had already spilled over the edges and begun searching for new paths and waterways. Some low-lying fields were filling with water. The ditches many farmers built to funnel water toward crops were now taxed with the liquid once providing life. The over-saturation would lead to obliteration.

In town, the water wound its way along narrow streets. The drainage system was no match for the water's force. Basement foundations were unable to keep the water-logged dirt and grasses from entering. Slowly, water seeped into homes providing muddy wading pools in places homeowners never dreamed of. Garages and lower-level rooms were teaming up with the storm and providing room for the water to pool. Sump pumps were no match for the waterlogged soil seeping into the privacy of homes.

***

Tom Rossiter's phone was rare to go off these days. Since retiring from the police force two years ago, he had been able to rest more easily at night without annoying texts waking him from restless slumber. But tonight was different. He knew from his days working in emergency management that many town leaders would be wide awake, eyes glued to news reports of the never-ending rain. Those in charge of the community had a responsibility to respond to the storm by providing warnings, shelter, and rescue. He simultaneously missed the excitement and was happy for the reprieve from the pressures of leading in times of crisis.

Tom hoped Gavin was wise enough to follow this story from somewhere warm and dry. He wanted to call Gavin but was all too aware that the two of them communicating had been less than minimal since his divorce from Gavin's mom, Melinda. Tom winced at the memory of his reckless affair with a dispatcher from work. Six years ago, Tom, like many men in transgressions often do, began to think more with his lower extremity than the one God put squarely on his shoulders. One night after work, he went to his lover's house and failed to turn his phone's locator off. He also failed to adequately persuade his son he was working a boring case late into the night. Instead, Gavin's curiosity got the best of him, and he decided to track his dad to see if he could determine what significant case Tom was working. Gavin always had it in his mind that the sleepy town of Bekkett was a festering pit of criminal activity. No matter how boring Tom insinuated his job usually was, Gavin continued to seek a worthy news story.

Tom later discovered Gavin used the family's phone locator, to determine his dad was not in town. It was rare for a Bekkett detective to work in the county's jurisdiction, so Gavin assumed there was a joint case with the sheriff's office, which had to be important. And because Tom had lied to Gavin, it piqued his curiosity even more. Throughout the evening, Gavin refreshed his phone to see if Tom's location would move. Of course, it remained in one fateful location.

As Tom continued to recall the events of that night, he looked out the window and shook his head with a slight smile considering the irony of how Tom's affair was brought to light. Using tools Tom taught Gavin on how to investigate, his son made one simple inquiry on the county assessor's website to see whose house Tom was now stationary at. Instead of finding the lead on a hot case, Gavin immediately recognized the owner's name of the property Tom had been at for far too long. He also knew the rumored reputation of said owner.

By the time Tom made it home, Gavin had become painfully aware of what was really going on behind his and his mom's backs. As Tom quietly snuck into his home, he was confronted by Gavin. To add to the misery, Gavin also made sure his mom was awake and present for the conversation. He wanted his dad to have no room for excuses or pleas for Gavin to keep this to themselves. As a result, Melinda packed one suitcase of clothes in the middle of the night two weeks later and disappeared. She left every possession behind, and Gavin's best investigative work never led him to his mom. Neither of the men had heard from her since that night. Tom's shame and embarrassment remained with him so many years later. Although he and Gavin made amends, he knew Gavin had never fully forgiven him and may never find it in himself to do so.

Now, standing in his living room, Tom looked out the window into a starless, cloudy night as large drops of rain smacked against the window. He closed his eyes, drew in a deep breath, held it, and listened to Mother Nature pour onto the roof and siding. He slowly released his breath and opened his eyes. He hoped the meditative breaths would calm his nerves. Instead, Tom found himself pacing and checking his phone every few minutes. Although he had retired his still employed friends often called during big cases for advice and he was hoping he would be called on again tonight. He wanted to be a part of this epic storm behind the scenes and in the know.

As if on cue, his phone chirped, and Tom quickly looked at the message. "Call the EOC ASAP. Backline. Gregg." It was his long-time friend and colleague. Tom and Gregg both retired from the police department the same year. Gregg did not enjoy long days at home working on chores around the house, so he went back to work part-time in the Emergency Operations Center. It sounded much fancier than it looked. The EOC was a joint training room, community room, and EOC. Federal grant money fed the ability to add phone lines, internet access, and eight TVs into a room that otherwise sat unused most days.

Tom had the number for the EOC still programmed in his speed dial and pushed the button to give Gregg a call. "Hello. Tom?" Gregg was expecting no other calls on this line. Not yet at least.

"Hey, it's me. What's going on? How can I help?" Tom was all too eager to lend a hand. Outside was brewing into an impressive storm and he wanted to be a part of the action.

"If you are not busy, we could use your years of experience working an emergency. The equipment's still the same and you know it as well as anyone. They say our main water source in the mountains is going to breech its banks around zero-three-hundred hours. Once that happens, it is impossible to tell where the water will move. Certainly, our direction. We need all hands on deck."

"Already dressed. Just waiting for your call. I'll be there in ten minutes. Thanks." Tom ran out the door not interested in wasting another minute.

September 14, 2013 – 1:15 AM

    Just outside of town, Jennifer awoke to a flash of lightning. Startled by the brightness that filled her room, she grabbed the edge of her sheet and pulled it tight against her neck and shoulders. A clap of thunder was followed by a slow rolling rumble that shuddered her bedroom walls. The eleven-year-old girl lay motionless in her bed willing the storm to pass so she could go back to sleep. She reminded herself of the words of her grandpa who told her the thunder was nothing more than the angels bowling in heaven. She took in a deep breath and exhaled slowly, calming her nerves.

    Jennifer lifted her head off her pillow just high enough to look at the foot of her bed. "Musket," she whispered. "Come here." Her dog needed no more invitation than her quiet, trembling voice. He stood up, turned in a circle, then made his way toward her face. Musket licked Jennifer on her right cheek, and she pulled her arm from the covers and rubbed the top of his head. With that, Musket plopped down with his rump against her shoulder. The two quietly allowed the night to pull them back to restful sleep.

September 13, 2013 – 1:30 AM

When Tom arrived at the Emergency Operations Center, he was amazed by the number of other people already hard at work laboring for solutions. He recognized a few, but many of his co-workers had also retired shortly after he left. The EOC was full of a lot of new young faces and Tom would have to remember he was here as a volunteer and could be asked to dump the trash for all he knew. Not that he would. He had more skills to offer that this small town was going to need to take advantage of.

Four large television screens were lit up with various newscasts from around the state. Weather maps shared the screen space and indicated no respite from the damp weather. Not for days. Already, the mountain communities were under mandatory evacuation. The sheriff's department had also extended the evacuation to outlying parts of the flat lands. Areas not far from the town limits.

Not finding Gregg, Tom knew the first task at hand was to determine the worst-case scenario for rising water levels and what neighborhoods might need to leave. Tom immediately went to the large worktable in the corner and pulled out the most recent city map. He turned to a young face he did not recognize and asked, "Can we have a topographical map over here?" Without waiting for an answer, he grabbed a red marker and began indicating the lowest lying areas on the meager map he had using his intimate knowledge of the layout of the town. One does not work the streets of Bekkett for twenty-seven years as a cop and not get to know every corner more than he would like. His rough estimate was evacuating 1,000 homes. At a minimum.

Tom pulled out his phone and thought it wise to let Gregg know he had arrived. He sent a quick text but would not leave his place at the map just yet.

***

Betty had settled into bed hours ago, but even the comfort of her sheets and quilt would not bring sleep. Her mind was racing with a thousand thoughts. At her age, she had hoped restless nights and wandering thoughts would not invade her mind. She had few worries or responsibilities and rarely experienced anything but rest after going to bed. But today's events were more significant than any she experienced in a long time. Betty stared wide-eyed at the ceiling. The digital alarm clock cast a faint glow in her room, and she studied the intricate design etched into the ceiling. Nearly a century ago, this room was added to the house and Joel Bekket used his craft as a carpenter to carve a rudimentary mountain scene into the ceiling. Betty studied the designs hoping it would distract her racing mind. It proved a fruitless way to fall asleep. Her thoughts continued to dance within the confines of her cranium.

Betty hoped sharing the journals with Marie was not a mistake. Her perception of Marie was of a woman seeking truthful answers, not as one to manipulate the story for her own gain. Betty silently prayed Marie would not bring a circus of media to Double K Ranch. Outside, the storm intensified, and Betty could not help but listen to the pounding rain with a bit of fear. In all her life on the ranch, she could not recall a storm as relentless as this. Her thoughts invaded her with the notion the moisture outside was permeating everything. Everywhere. She only hoped the crypt could withstand this storm. It must, or infamy would be rained upon Double K Ranch when the knowledge was finally discovered of this horrendous family secret.

September 13, 2013 – 2:15 AM

Twenty miles west of Bekkett was the town's primary water source. Three thousand feet higher than the town's elevation, lay Peaceful Waters Reservoir. In 1922, town leaders recognized the need for a continuous water resource and began scouting for the perfect location to build a dam and create a lake. One such scouting party trekked two miles off the highway, following a small stream to locate its source. They crested a hill and found a beautiful meadow valley at the base of three mountain peaks. It was the ideal landscape for town engineers to build a dam. The runoff from the nearby peaks, coupled with generous mountain streams, fed the thirsty meadow, eventually creating the reservoir. A series of valves and gates kept the control of the flow of water downstream and onto the plains around Bekkett in the hands of the engineers.

The ferocity of the present situation with this storm's persistence pushed the industrial ingenuity from nearly a century ago to its limit. The collected rain combined with the runoff from nearby melting snow finally caused the Peaceful Waters Reservoir to succumb to the rising water. The last restraint in place to hold back a torrent of liquid was failing. The lake climbed over the dam and pressed downstream with such force, little could stand in its path. The riverbed at the base of the reservoir had been reinforced in the late 1940s with concrete walls after that era's great storm. In comparison to today, it caused minimal devastation but was strong enough to bring the Army Corps of

Engineers in to make improvements for sustaining the rushing waters within its channel.

But at the intersection where Peaceful Waters River merged with Dry Creek, two enemies conspired together to form one alliance. A powerful alliance with authority and influence to mete out punishment without discussion. At the joining of these two waterways, they became one river flowing into Bekkett's Sand Creek. And it was Sand Creek which would soon devour all in its path like a carnivore coming off a three day fast.

***

Today, the dam was operated remotely from a control center miles away. Alarms activated in the Emergency Operations Center indicating the dam failed at its job. The darkness of night obscured the video cameras from capturing the volatility of the situation. Operators investigated from afar but were unprepared for the seriousness of the state of the dam. Only after seeing the deluge from the sky and continued forecasts was the veracity of this situation understood. It was only a matter of time before the decision makers of Bekkett lost all ability to move people.

"We need reverse 911 calls to all homes along Sand Creek. One half mile in each direction!" Gregg yelled at the communications center. "The school has already offered us their buses. They will be at various points within fifteen minutes. Tell the residents to get to the buses or drive away immediately! This is not voluntary!"

The problem with predicting future outcomes is the inability to remain accurate in your calculations. It is educated guessing, at best. Gregg knew they were making some good guesses, but something in his gut told him this was not going to be as easy as it appeared on paper. Gregg had already perused the markings Tom made on the topographical map and agreed with Tom's assessment. Still, he felt uneasy inside.

He pulled Tom aside, "I don't like this," he said. "I feel like we're missing something. Like all hell is about to break loose and we're bound and gagged."

Tom had felt the same sixth sense one gets when trouble looms in the shadows. "I know what you mean. This just feels..." Tom was not sure how to finish that sentence, nor did he need to.

"I know. Hard to describe," Gregg filled the pause.

September 13, 2013 – 3:15 AM

Betty gave up on trying to sleep. Something was tugging at her thoughts, and it was keeping her from rest. She got out of bed and donned her robe and slippers. Moving into the kitchen, she caught a reflection in the window that caused her to stop in her tracks. She turned her head toward the window and saw it again. Movement. Someone, or worse, something, was moving just outside her house. It almost appeared to be dancing in a rhythmic fashion.

Daring to get a better look, Betty stepped to the window and put her face against the pane. With the combination of the clouds, the rain, and the tree cover, light was not penetrating into her yard. Betty reluctantly flipped on the exterior light. She felt both afraid the light would yell her position to the 'thing' outside and hopeful the light would cause it to flee.

She closed her eyes momentarily. When she opened them, she was not expecting the sight that met her failing vision. What she had seen moving outside was the creek which had crested over its banks. Not by a mere few inches. It was lapping at the foundation of her house. As the water fed off the structure, she realized her house would no longer have the strength to resist the water's surge. Betty glanced toward her car and realized her fear was rising in syncopation with the water. The car was mostly submerged. She was trapped. One route of escape was all she could think of.

Without thought of the fact she was only wearing her nightgown, robe, and slippers, Betty headed toward the back door. If she could get outside through that door, she only had to walk fifteen feet before she could get to higher ground. It would provide her another thirty feet in elevation. Surely that would be more than enough to stave off this rising tide.

Betty made it up the field, slipping once and soiling her robe with the muddy field she was trotting through. She was suddenly overcome with fear thinking about her ancient relative, Luke. Were the conditions similar to this on the last night he walked this earth? How near to his last footsteps was she now standing? Would her fate be the same as his?

She had to push those thoughts aside and focus on survival.

***

"Check this out, Gavin!" Marie nearly screamed.

"What?"

"Well, based on what your drunken rambler said in those stories you found today at the library, and based on this journal entry, there may be some credence to his tale. This is the first time this journal is beginning to speak of more beastly ideas!" Marie was deeply passionate about her discovery.

As Gavin pulled his chair closer, Marie continued, "So far, the journal was only explaining about the Bekkett journey to this area from back east. It was mainly stuff I already knew. But then there's some information about some guy named Weston. Unfortunately, that is where the journal pages slipped out. The ones you tried to save from the rain. Any luck with those, by the way?"

Gavin had been meticulously working with them in the bathroom with a dryer. He had not had any luck. The ink had run so drastically, no words could be salvaged. "Unfortunately, I'm afraid those pages may be lost for good."

"How could I have been so impatient? If I had made sure the satchel was closed, that would never have happened. How am I going to explain to Betty I ruined three, if not more, pages of her family journal?" Marie said.

Trying to deflect some of her anger back to excitement Gavin asked, "What were you going to tell me you found?"

Marie continued, "Well, I think a lot of time passed because I don't know who Weston is. I never heard of him before. But the pages in the journal are speaking of a bear-like animal eating the chickens on the ranch. Even more exciting is an entry about a traveler who came to Bekkett and apparently had his horse eaten, so he claims.

"The journal says some guy, apparently a guest to the region, had been rambling on about some intense screaming he had heard in the middle of the day. A day described as stormy, overcast, and pelting down rain. This visitor spoke about a missing pack of horses – a large monetary loss to any ranch hand in those days. What was most curious was the lack of concern among the old-timers in town. As if it were a common occurrence to lose 10 horses.

"A few nights later, this visitor was at the saloon when he ran into a drunk patron whose whiskey caused his lips to get a little too loose. The drunkard droned on about a beast and about its appetite for blood when it rained down from above. The drunkard told the visitor it was the town's secret, and they fed the beast's appetite by feeding it animals – better than its desire to chew on human flesh."

Gavin had a blank stare. "Don't you get it? The beast is real!" Marie exclaimed.

"I think the Bekkett's had more knowledge about the beast than they liked to admit. Whoever wrote the journal entry also says they later put a bullet in the head of both the visitor and the drunkard." Marie's words trailed off as she tried to grasp how horrible one would have to be to kill two people for merely speaking about a mythical creature. Yet she also couldn't believe one would murder over a made-up relic. *It must be real* she thought.

***

Betty heard the noise in the distance. Like a thousand bees buzzing by her head all at one time. It was the most out of place and unknown sound she had ever heard. In the midst of a storm pelting rain into the muddy field, she wasn't focused on the patter at her feet, but the assault on her ears. The sound was rattling her ear drums causing her to swat at her head to make it stop. As the noise intensified, she closed her eyes and strained her neck in several directions to determine what it was. She looked down to focus on the audible noise. Unable to determine its source, she opened her eyes. She was startled to see ripples of water dancing around her ankle. The water was on the rise.

For the first time in her life, Betty realized she was near death. She chuckled. *Funny. I always thought that darn beast would resurrect and kill me, the keeper of its dungeon. I never thought I would drown.* The water could not be contained. Betty was too weak to move quickly. She knew there was only one direction to go for higher ground. She began to walk toward the plot of ground where her family built its underground secret. Within this dungeon, the beast lay, hopefully, dry and undisturbed in his ancient crypt. As Betty traversed toward the tomb, the water inched up quickly. It was up to her knees and then her waist within just mere minutes.

Lord, protect this town. Forgive me for keeping so many secrets. Kill the beast. Just before the weight of the water pushed her onto her back, Betty heard a scream like none she had ever heard before. Her eyes popped wide open at the realization of what she heard. A sound she had only imagined from all the stories. As she began to comprehend her truest fear, the river ganged up on her and pushed her under its surface.

September 14, 2013 – 4:00 AM

The water had moved downstream with calculation. What had been unforeseen was the force it brought as it swept away deep-rooted trees, boulders the size of small cars and well-established houses nestled perilously close to the water's edge. It was tearing away at the ground without mercy. Destruction was all it knew. Pushing away from the natural banks, the river created new lanes of travel. Berms meant to protect property quickly met their capacity and were unable to distract the water toward the left or right. Waves of dirt and mud rode on top of this never-before-seen tide of water. Boundaries were broken. The rivers had created one massive torrent of devastation. Neither the size nor weight of objects in the water's path had any consideration. Obliviation was imminent.

At the north boundary of the Double K Ranch, the river bent in a natural arc around the rise of the field. Tonight, however, the river created a new channel. With the force of a small army, the water dug into terra firma and exposed soil that had never seen the sun. This new path led to the piece of land holding a decades old secret. A crypt. A buried dungeon that held stories of terror, fear, and death. A tomb that held a defeated beast from long ago. Within this void, under the field, the Bekkett's farmed for a century hid a secret they had planned on never being discovered. Never being disturbed.

The river pounded into the side of the crypt. The layers of dirt, stones and grass that had been painstakingly molded together to keep water at bay were now muddy remnants of history. The tomb within was pushed into the opposite wall, crushing the last defense against evil resurrecting from its grave. As water pounded into the crypt, the tomb shot to the surface like an inflatable craft that had been held underwater against its will for too long. The force with which it shot erect from the water's surface launched it high into the night air. Gravity grabbed ahold of the wooden tomb, forcing it back to earth, and slamming the tomb against a tree limb of formidable size. The aged wood of the tomb was brittle and unable to withstand such blunt-force trauma. It splintered apart exposing an oilcloth wrapped object. An object that had been conjured from the depths of hell itself.

The oilcloth soaked up the river which permeated into the flesh of the beast that had been wrapped within. Drenching it to its core, life sprung into the beast's lungs. One could suppress evil momentarily, but it would take much more than man-made encrusting to keep evil at bay forever.

September 14, 2013 – 4:30 AM

Steve Laycock had been up since two thirty a.m. His church, Rising Son Fellowship, was a designated Red Cross shelter and he received a wakeup call from the Emergency Operations Center during the darkness of night. He was informed evacuations were about to become mandatory for thousands of residents and his church needed to set up shelter. Steve immediately called a cadre of pre-determined volunteers to assist in setting up cots and pulling blankets from the three sheds on the church property that housed shelter supplies. Nearly two hours after that phone call, he finally had a moment to sit in his office reclining chair, sip on some coffee and think.

After Haiti's devastating four hurricanes in 2008, Steve and many other aid workers traveled to the island to assist in recovery efforts. He knew all too well the immense power water could have on a home. As he pictured the ruined homesteads from Haiti in his mind, he prayed for safe passage for those fleeing today and the protection of their properties. Although it may be material in nature, he knew the value of personal belongings and the memories they held. *God divert the water to areas without homes. Protect our town. And may the stories of the Bekkett Beast be folklore.*

As soon as Steve silently prayed his last sentence, he felt foolish. *How could a man who serves God each day buy into such silly nonsense? How could I, of all people, believe some mythical creature was created by someone other than God with its sole existence designed to terrorize?* Laughing and shaking his head, Steve knew he could indeed believe such a tale. He had personally seen the power of evil at work in the lives of a few Haitian villagers. Until he had visited this distant land, he had only heard the stories of voodoo religious practices. But being there, among the natives, he saw firsthand the power some Haitians gave to the spirits of their voodoo master, Loa. When he came home and spoke of Loa to those in his congregation, all admitted they envisioned Haitians with little dolls designed to inflict pain on their enemies. Years of Hollywood dramatization of voodoo dolls sustained this false notion.

Steve saw Loa for what it really was. He had talked face-to-face with practitioners of their age-old religion. He knew Simbi and Kouzin Zaka were spirits of rain and agriculture. Therefore, it made sense that, even here in America, a beast conjured to produce rain for life-giving agriculture, was a possibility. Far-fetched and highly unlikely. But possible. One does not name a spirit if it is only a fairy tale. Names are given to those who are valued. Or worshipped.

***

Two years earlier, Betty Bekkett began attending Rising Son Fellowship. At the time, Steve thought little of the new addition to his congregation. It was status-quo to have people come and go. But Betty remained. She was silent but dedicated toward volunteer work. She played a vital role in the church becoming a Red Cross shelter. Donations were spear-headed by Betty and her contagious spirit prompted others to equally contribute supplies even though it was unheard of for a church in this locale to become a shelter when there were very few disasters regionally.

Yet her work, communication with Red Cross leaders, and persistence became the sole reason for the preparedness the church now had in the current crisis. Had Betty not led the charge, Rising Son would be a fading shadow as the waters rose and people begged for refuge. Steve allowed her to work on the endeavor not giving it much thought at first. Many people, especially in the end stages of life, want to make a difference and know they are leaving a legacy. However, this was personal for Betty. Steve was curious.

As Steve and Betty worked together more closely, she began to confide in him more and more. Just two days ago, after celebrating the one-year anniversary of the church's acquisition of cots, blankets, and emergency supplies, Betty asked to speak with Steve in private. *Here we go,* he said to himself. *She is going to confess her sins and finally explain her passion for this mission.* He never imagined what she was going to tell him. At the time, Steve was sure the tale she wove and her knowledge of the Bekkett family secret were clear indications of her failing mind, overcome by insanity and old age. He had muffled a scoffing tone more than once as she spoke. Today, however, he reflected on her passion and conviction and was beginning to believe her narrative. Maybe she had not been lying, misled, or ravaged by dementia. *Was it possible every act of preparation was for this moment in time?* If so, he feared beds and food would do nothing more than fuel the fury of this great unknown creature.

***

Steve stood and stretched his tired body. Headlights were shining into his office and he knew those fleeing disaster were seeking shelter. As Steve walked down the hallway toward the vestibule he could not rid himself of the notion that today would produce evil events. He shook his head trying to dislodge the thoughts from his dark shaggy head of hair as if they were flecks of dandruff. He entered the main lobby, turned on his vivacious smile and reached out to shake hands of those wandering into the church. He directed many toward the gymnasium, which became the ad hoc kitchen and living room, where many were beginning to set up their home away from home.

As pastors so eloquently do, he made the rounds and met with those pouring in. Seeking to understand their circumstances he asked questions and was overcome with sympathy at their plight. He was told how so many at the base of the mountains heeded the flash flood warning and fled with only a few moment's notice. In their desperation to survive, they brought with them only a few essentials as they pulled on clothes and hunted for car keys. In the cover of night, the ferocity of the water could not be comprehended. As people drove fearfully to safer ground, they were forced to trust the authorities' accuracy in having them flee in haste. As they sat in the shelter of the church, tears fell at the realization they possessed nothing more than what they could carry in their arms. Pictures and family heirlooms would be lost and memories would be the only sustaining hope.

September 14, 2013 – 5:00 AM

The beast used its power to pull itself from the torrent. Looking around, the terrain was unfamiliar and somehow it knew it had been in captivity for over a century. The beast smirked at being held down temporarily, never permanently. It fed on the terror of its prey. Turning its head to sniff the air the creature smelled the cornucopia of fear emanating from its surroundings. Created by the greed of man and driven by its need for life giving rain, the beast was lusting for blood. Rain soaked into the monster's every pore, demanding its appetite be satiated. Its capability to hunt and move unseen was enhanced with the drenching of the ground. Mud encased the beast in obscurity, blinding mankind to its existence. The inability of the beast's prey to perceive its presence would allow it to devour flesh easily.

Out of the corner of its left eye was movement. Not that of a human. A small animal wandering toward its inevitable death. The beast froze as the brown, rain-soaked life form happily ran toward it. This critter's innocence would be its demise. *Animals are stupid. Running toward their death as if it were playtime,* the beast thought. With a thoughtless lunge, the beast overtook the small dog. Carefully examining its meal, the beast gripped the canine in its talons. *Someone will miss you which makes this minuscule meal more savory.* Slowly, the beast crushed the dog's lungs until the whimpering ceased. Equally as slowly, the beast gave slight relief to tease the animal into thinking the hurried breaths it inhaled would continue. The beast only allowed the dog to breathe so its whining could be heard. *Your cries sustain me, you foul animal.*

Then, slowly, with the dog tightly grasped, the beast began to peel off the furry outer layer. Its meal produced a sorrowful, ear piercing sound the beast desired. *Yes!!!* At first, the beast matched the intensity of the dog's shrieks. Once matched in tone, the beast opened its mouth wide, lifted its head into the falling rain, and continued to scream. A shrill, loud yell none in this century had ever heard. The terror it caused his listeners soothed the appetite of the beast. The shrieking continued until pain overtook the animal and it slumped lifeless in the grasp of the beast. This first meal would prove to be nothing more than an appetizer created for a small child. It craved more blood. More meat. The hunt would continue.

September 14, 2013 – 6:15 AM

The sun would be breaching the horizon within the hour. Ahead of its arrival, the night sky was already beginning to acquiesce its blinding darkness. The school buses had barely been used. Only the elderly seemed to take advantage of the public transportation the town officials had provided for the evacuation. Most of the residents were too obstinate to heed the warnings. Those fortunate enough to leave were taken to Rising Son Fellowship for shelter.

Now that a myriad of residents were pulled from their sleep, they became spectators to the falling rain and the rising water. To the truly foolish, this poised an opportunity to inflate some tubes and take a trip down the river's waterway. Only during spring run-off was the water depth enough to enjoy water activities on Sand Creek. The town hosted annual tubing parties, but this was no time to entertain oneself on the water. It was rising too quickly and moving unpredictably outside of its banks. Emergency operators were ill-equipped and understaffed to deal with those who purposefully chose to play with danger.

Tom & Gregg were receiving periodic updates from the men and women on the police force working overtime to stay ahead of the storm. All they could do from the EOC was shake their heads and work even more diligently to warn these fools. More pre-recorded messages were created telling people to shelter indoors and to not go near the unpredictable water.

"If I weren't so used to the stupidity of some people, I'd probably be shocked," Tom said to Gregg.

"I know. It's what kept you employed for so many years. It's what keeps the entire police force today working. In a way, we need them," Gregg replied.

"I'd be happy if everyone woke up tomorrow with an abundance of common sense and grace toward others. I'd gladly have retired earlier if that had been the case years ago," Tom sighed.

"You? Retire earlier? Right. That's why you're here now. Because you want to get away from this type of work," Gregg said with truthful sarcasm.

"Touché," Tom laughed.

***

Gavin looked toward Marie's window. Only then did he realize she had blackout blinds drawn. He stood up and pulled the cord revealing the gray world outside. The rain was still falling. The sun was still hiding. Gavin rubbed his eyes and wished he had the chance to get even a few minutes of sleep. He knew he did not behave well when he was too tired. Or hungry. Now he was both.

Once Marie had nodded off to sleep, he pulled out his maps. He cleared an area on her floor and laid out the pages he had printed. He focused only on the area with the elevation and where he had seen Betty ascending from what he could only guess was some sort of catacomb. He carefully taped each page together so there was no white border to separate the pages. Unfortunately, the map, as meticulous as it was, offered little in answers.

He then downloaded his pictures onto Marie's 22" monitor where he could more carefully scrutinize the photos he had captured the day before. When he zoomed in on Betty, he saw she was holding the journals in her hand. They, apparently, had been stored underground. Maybe that portion of land was nothing more than a storm shelter turned storage room. Without full access to it, there was no way to know what other secrets it may be hiding.

Gavin looked back into the apartment and saw Marie was still sleeping on her sofa. She was sitting in the corner, knees tucked toward her chin. Her head was resting on the high back cushions behind her. Staring at her beauty, he wished he could wake each morning to see Marie silently slumbering. He walked across the small room toward Marie, when he noticed one of the journals lying open next to her. He quietly approached her and picked up the journal. Flipping through a few pages, he found himself glued to one entry.

April 10, 1870

I crossed Mr. Wilson's field today. Took a short-cut to town. I know it's frowned upon by Pa, but so many things are, I tend to not care anymore. As I ran down Wilson's hill, I stumbled and rolled part way down. When I came to rest, I was face to face with mutilation. Nearly soiled my pants! I think it had been a bovine. Its flesh was gone. Pieces of blood soaked carcass were buzzing with flies. I jumped up and fell backward. Pretty sure that's when I threw up. The sight was gruesome. I stood and looked around. Two legs were still attached to the rotting body. Another leg was about five feet away. The skull was all that was left untouched. Eyes boring into nothing – staring into the ground where its blood and guts now soaked. Up till now I only heard the tales. The fearful stories passed down from grandma. Part of me always wondered if they were true. I know it now. I also know she spared me all the details. In all the stories she told, none had me picturing this kind of feast. In all my days, I hope to never see that again. I hope to never end life as that poor cow did.

"Holy crap!" Gavin exclaimed a bit louder than he intended, while simultaneously tossing the journal back onto the sofa.

"What?" Marie asked as if she had been watching him the entire time. The frog in her throat betrayed the fact she had just woken up.

Gavin handed the journal to Marie and pointed to the page he had just read. "I can honestly say, I wasn't ready to believe the reality of what you've been hunting. Now, I don't want to know anymore. This is all too crazy. Do you know who wrote that?"

Marie took the journal from Gavin. She placed her thumb on the page he had pointed to and then flipped the journal closed. She then opened the front cover and looked inside. "This is a journal Luke wrote, I'm guessing. His name was written inside the front cover. I think someone else later wrote family names on all or most of the journals. Smart move."

Gavin turned and walked into the kitchen. He opened Marie's cupboards until he found what he was searching for. Coffee. And filters. He needed a strong cup of java to help him wrap his weary mind around this horrific discovery. Needing to change the subject, Gavin called into the other room, "Do you want anything to eat? I'm going to make eggs and toast. Might as well make two servings."

"That would be great. Thanks, Gavin." Marie replied.

Gavin whipped some eggs and milk into a creamy texture while he allowed a butter-soaked pan to heat up. He poured the eggs into the pan and could not help but wonder where this discovery was headed. Would they tell anyone? Would anyone even believe them? The scrambled eggs Gavin cooked reminded him his mind was feeling a bit scrambled as well.

Needing to gain some focus, Gavin spoke up, turning his head toward Marie. "Where's your toaster?"

"In the cabinet by your right knee."

Gavin bent down and pulled the appliance off the shelf and placed it on the counter. He opened a few more cabinets searching for bread. While searching he said, "Hey. Check out the map on the floor. Better yet, look at the pictures on your computer. Tell me what you see." He was hoping she may find something he had missed. "Maybe you can make sense of it all."

"Alright, but I'm not sure what you are hoping I may find."

"Neither am I."

Marie spent the next few minutes scanning the documents. The paper map was nicely put together but offered little value to Marie. She stared quizzically at it for a few minutes, then turned to her computer. "Is that Betty standing in her field?"

"Sure is."

"What is she doing?"

"I zoomed in earlier. She's holding those journals in her hands. I think she has a storage container below ground out in her field."

"I bet that's where she was going to take me if it hadn't been raining. She said she was going to show me something, but then changed her mind. As soon as this rain lets up, we need to go straight to her ranch."

In the kitchen, Gavin buttered the toast and scooped eggs onto two plates. He set the table for two and poured the freshly brewed coffee. "Breakfast's ready, Marie. Take a break and come enjoy."

"Thanks. Smelling those eggs got my stomach growling."

Sitting across from Marie, Gavin took a bite, quickly swallowed and asked, "What is this beast? Do you think it is really possible that it's still wandering the mountains today feeding off of cougars and other wild animals? Or..." Gavin paused. "Or is it possible, somehow the Bekketts captured the beast?" With more hesitation and a questioning tone, Gavin added, "Maybe that's what Betty's hiding underground?"

When Marie said nothing, Gavin continued his dialogue. "I gotta admit. I'm both extremely intrigued and a bit in shock. I *really* thought this was a wild goose chase. But there is no way this guy Luke, over one hundred years ago, was writing this stuff down with the intent of just freaking out future generations. This has to be real." Trying to get Marie to say something, he asked, "Did you see anything on those maps that makes any sense?"

"Sorry. I missed a bit of what you were saying. I was thinking of Betty holding those journals.

"Ignoring me already?" Gavin said with feigned hurt. "I get it. There is so much to soak in. I was just speculating as to where this thing may be at right now," Gavin added for clarification.

"Not ignoring you. Just thinking. For whatever reason, the beast seemed to remain in this general region. Which means if it is alive today, it is probably not in the mountains. It was this community's personal nightmare. No other community in the area has ever shared stories of a beast or mutilated animals. Trust me, I looked." Marie did not provide any more information, but silently agreed the dungeon on the ranch may hold the beast. Or at least it's carcass. Instead of saying more, she focused on eating. As she took a bite of her eggs, she realized this was the first time in more than 12 hours she had eaten.

"You know how to cook. I know they are just eggs, but you have a special touch. I have never been able to achieve fluffy eggs like you only see on commercials. These have got to rival those of Aunt B's," Marie said, referring to the best diner in town.

"Well, I did learn from the best. I actually worked for Jackie for a while over at Aunt B's. She taught me quite a bit about getting around in the kitchen." Little had Gavin known in those days of cooking just to make ends meet would someday result in impressing a woman. Oh, how the little things in life seem to have more significance than you realize in the moment. Marie and Gavin finished breakfast and sipped on their morning coffee allowing a few minutes of silence to pass. Gavin was grateful the silence was not filled with that normal sense of awkwardness found in new friendships.

Gavin quizzed Marie further and asked, "What else did you discover last night?"

"It is almost overwhelming trying to put order and sanity into this whole thing," Marie replied. "As best I can tell, the drought from 1845 to 1847 caused great devastation to the region. I already knew that, but the journals seem to confirm its veracity. The drought was killing the local crops and farmers in the area began to leave for more fertile land. This is about where the journals get scrambled. But it seems a group of settlers from back east are a topic of interest. With that group was someone described as a witch. As best as I can tell, after their arrival it started raining."

"So, she was the Lord of the Rain?" Gavin laughed at his own dad joke.

Marie groaned at his comment. "Sounds like something my dad would have said."

"You're welcome!" Gavin said.

"To continue," Marie added, "it was after the rain began again that more journal entries speak of all the carnage in the region. It adds credence to the story of the guy in the bar spewing about the beast killing his animals." Marie hesitated then slowly added, "I think your Lord of the Rain... may have... created the beast."

"What?!" Gavin said incredulously. "That's silly talk. I think your sleep deprived mind is getting the better of you."

Marie quickly changed subjects out of fear of Gavin arguing with her. After all, she would not have any way to prove her suspicions. "Have you ever been to Israel?" she asked Gavin.

"Nope, can't say that I have nor have any desire to travel to the Middle East," he replied. "That was a sudden change of topic," he added.

"Not completely. Let me explain. How familiar are you with the Bible?" Marie asked.

"Well, I've gone to church, off and on, most my life. I have read, or at least skimmed, most of the Bible at least once. I tend to focus on the New Testament. Why?"

Marie continued, "All I knew about this beast as a child were the stories told in secret. But it was explained the beast came out only during rainstorms. I thought little of that when I was a child. It always seemed to be a way to keep kids inside during storms, so parents did not have to deal with little muddy, wet footprints being tracked inside. But this whole thing is starting to make a bit more sense when I think of my trip to Israel."

"Okay. So how do Israel and the Bible connect us to the Bekkett Beast?" Gavin wondered aloud.

"Fertility!" Marie exclaimed a bit too enthusiastically. "The rain brought life to the crops in Bekkett. And the crops were vital to sustain life to those who lived in and around the region."

"Okay. And…?" Gavin prodded.

"The Israelites moved into the Promised Land after they left Egypt. Do you remember that?" she asked trying to keep Gavin engaged.

"Yep. They wandered for forty years in the desert, as I recall. Not super fertile if you ask me," Gavin said.

"Exactly. They wandered in dry terrain being fed manna as a means to rid themselves of Egyptian culture and worship. God needed them to turn their focus toward Him so they could truly appreciate their relocation. They were moving into now foreign territory. The area had been populated by the Canaanites and others while the Israelites had been held captive for five hundred years by the Egyptians."

"Five hundred years?" Gavin asked.

"Give or take a century," Marie replied. "The point is, despite God warning the Israelites time and time again to destroy all the idols of the foreigners, the Israelites just could not follow through. They had been surrounded by another culture and other religions for centuries. It is not easy to simply rid oneself of old habits. Does that make sense?"

"Yes. I can relate," Gavin replied.

"One of the idols they continued to worship and allowed to remain intact was the Asherah Pole. Ring a bell, Bible scholar?" Marie playfully asked.

"I remember Baal was a common idol they worshipped," Gavin answered. "But I can't say the Asherah Pole stands out as a topic of Sunday School discussion."

"If you know Baal, then you are only a step away from Asherah. She is believed to be Baal's mom. Quite the role model if I say so. She was worshiped as the goddess of fertility. Asherah Poles were often built in dry climates or during dry seasons. Their worship was a despicable act of sexual orgies, but it was also a ritual to promote rain and the growth of crops. When I was in Israel, some of the poles were still erect. And phallic in stature," Marie explained. She could go on but feared boring Gavin and distracting him from her main point. And she wanted to avoid using the words sexual orgy, erect, and phallic around Gavin again. Awkward.

"Oh," was all Gavin could muster.

Wanting to move on Marie quickly continued. "Anyway, since Asherah Poles represented fertility and we are guessing the Bekkett Beast came to life during a dry time, it now seems more like a modern-day Canaanite idol. It would be plausible to say the Bekkett Beast and Asherah Poles represent the same thing. Except our beast has far more gruesome consequences than... Canaanite rituals," she carefully said to avoid bringing the topic of sex up again.

"Nice explanation, but I just can't see some old batty lady wandering into Bekkett and creating some beast out of nothingness so the locals could grow crops again. That is too Stephen King for me. And what's in it for the old lady anyways?" Gavin said.

"That's part of the mystery! I was hoping these journals would contain answers. That's why I'm most intrigued with this guy Weston. I've never heard of him before and I'm betting he plays a bigger role in all of this than any of us realize." *Not that anyone realizes anything related to the beast*, Marie thought.

Marie reached over to Gavin's plate and used her fork to steal his last bite of eggs. "Good stuff! Now, grab your phone, and let's get outta here. I've got keys to the library and the alarm automatically disarmed at six this morning. I wanna find out who Weston is."

"I dug through everything yesterday. Don't recall reading about anyone named Weston."

"Then you didn't look hard enough. I love history so much partly because no one in this town has ever had the courage to throw anything away. Bekkett's history is most definitely stored in the library. Every word of it."

"Except those journals, Marie. Those were not in the library. Maybe Betty is hiding more info in that dungeon of hers. Maybe she only gave you enough to keep you off her back for the next couple of weeks while she doctored some other journals to provide some false documentation. Ever thought of that?" Gavin taunted.

"Then we'll drive on over to the Double K and bust into that dungeon ourselves! Something I may choose to do anyway," Marie said as she walked out her front door. Gavin was left with no choice but to follow her lead.

September 14, 2013 – 7:15 AM

    Taylor woke up early. Laying under the covers did not hide the light filtering into his room from the windows. Someday, he may actually choose productivity over laziness and buy some window coverings. Probably not today. In fact, today he may not be able to leave the property. He had been watching the rain fall and the creek rise all day yesterday. It was the most excitement he had out here. Living with his friends who had to fly around the world on extended business trips was not tough work. They provided him a place to stay in return for maintaining their farm each day. Other than a few hunting excursions on the surrounding property, Taylor didn't get out much.

    Sauntering upstairs into the kitchen, Taylor never acquired his tastebuds for the fine dining experience his friends were clearly accustomed to. He let the squid and lobster tails remain in the freezer, while he much preferred something he could zap in the microwave or grab out of the fruit basket. But he did enjoy their selection of caffeine. Brewing a warm cup of espresso, he sat at the granite countertop and flipped on the satellite TV. He peeled a banana and watched the weather forecast. Seems the local dam was breached overnight, and the water along the creek was definitely going to rise. All homes along Sand Creek were under mandatory evacuation and most of Bekkett was prepared to leave at a moment's notice.

    Taylor looked down at his phone. He hadn't received any evacuation notices. There was no landline into the house and no way for the authorities to know it was his cell phone that should be alerted. It was then Taylor glanced up from the television and looked outside for the first time that morning. Although the property bordered the creek, the house itself was 75 yards away and on a hilltop overlooking the winding creek. No chance of flooding from this perch. It would be a front row seat to some serious riptides, but Taylor was sure he'd stay dry up here.

He sauntered to the wall-length window for a closer look. Surveilling the outdoors, he noticed the field surrounding the house was now a lake. Despite the fact someone else was probably having a bad day, the enormity and grandeur of this sight was impressive. Already, Taylor was thinking of the Jet Ski he knew was in the barn out back. He saw an opportunity in his near future for some previously un-thought-of water sports.

Taylor decided to further scope out the clearly changed landscape. His friends were astronomy freaks, hence the large glass panes that encompassed the southwest facing wall. Two telescopes were perched nearby, one large telescope clearly designed for viewing distant galaxies. The other a perfect size to scope out much closer objects. Taylor pressed his eye to the lens of the smaller telescope and angled its view in the direction of the water's surface. He focused his gaze on the western edge of the property. The fence was no longer visible. In its place was a slight bulge in the flowing water.

Following the rise in the water along a straight line, he determined the fence must be just under the surface. The current of the water flowing through the barbs was creating small rapids just above the fence line. Looking toward the northwest corner, the highest point along the fence, he could see the top of one of the fence posts sticking above the water's edge. Around it, debris was beginning to pile up. Nature was building itself a dam.

Taylor was overrun with fascination at the force of the water. This house had been transformed into lakefront property in a matter of hours. Taylor left the scope, went outside, and walked the perimeter of the house on the three-hundred-and-sixty-degree elevated porch. It was clear, there was no leaving the house now. It had been surrounded by water on all sides. Taylor would rely on nature to keep the water at bay. The pantry was stocked and the animals in the barn had plenty of their own food. He was well prepared to hunker down and stay put.

September 14, 2013 – 8:00 AM

Jennifer awoke drenched in her own sweat. She had remained swallowed in her blanket's cocoon of fear after last night's storm had shaken her awake. She flipped back the covers and the air in her room felt like an arctic breeze as it touched her damp skin. Jennifer rubbed the sleep from her eyes and was grateful for the light shining through her thin curtains. She opened the curtains hoping for rays of sunlight to brighten her mood but was greeted instead by low-hanging gray clouds.

Hearing her parents downstairs, she looked around for Musket to corral him out of her bedroom. She had fallen asleep again while Musket pressed his fury body against her side in a show of comfort. Musket was the family dog with beautiful dark brown puppy dog eyes, and she loved it when he chose to sleep on her bed. He brought comfort and peace even though he was much more dog by name than character. Usually, his 15-pound frame was curled in a ball in the sunbeams on the soft carpet. Occasionally, he did a trick or two, but he really preferred the pampered life on someone's lap. Her family laughed about Musket being more cat-like than dog.

Jennifer rounded the corner into the kitchen and saw her parents packing pictures into boxes.

"Why are you packing? Are we moving?" Jennifer asked with shock in her voice. And a bit of relief at the thought of leaving the isolation of their secluded home.

"No. Well, yes. Sort of. Temporarily." Her mom said, obviously a bit flustered.

Jennifer looked toward her dad who filled in the gaps. "We have to leave the house for a while. The creek is overflowing, and we have been told if we don't evacuate our house we could get trapped here or swallowed by the water."

"Gary, don't be so forthright," Jennifer's mom said to her husband. "You'll scare Jennifer."

"I'm already scared. I've never really liked it here, and you know that," Jennifer replied. "Besides, I understand about water and flooding. What should I pack?"

"We only have about thirty minutes, honey. Just get your phone, some pictures, and your memory book."

"And Musket," Jennifer added.

"Of course. Musket too," Jennifer's mom agreed.

"Where is Musket, anyways?" Jennifer asked, looking around the ground level of the house. "I haven't seen him since last night."

"Well, he came into our room sometime in the middle of the night. I guess I remember hearing him jump off the bed about four this morning," Jennifer's mom recalled. "Check outside. But do not go any further than the fenced yard. The water level is too unpredictable further out."

"Okay. I'll be careful."

Jennifer walked out of the sliding glass door and shut it behind her. She looked down to her left and saw the dog door, silently hoping Musket hadn't used it to go outside in the middle of the night.

"Musket! Musket! Here, boy!" Jennifer called out. Her words were muffled by the pattering of the rain. "Musket!" She waited a full five minutes then walked the exterior fence line. She called out to him every few feet, but he did not come bounding to her like he usually did when he heard her melodic voice beckoning him home.

Jennifer reluctantly walked back inside the house. Her tears and water-soaked face melded into one sorrowful flow of emotions. Living in the country had taught her something. Never get too attached. The wild animals loved a good meal. This would be her third pet to never walk home. But this time was worse than the others. She cringed at the thought of Musket being swept away by the rushing river. She was done having pets.

September 14, 2013 – 8:10 AM

Gavin had been a lot of places in this town pursuing journalistic leads and stories. But he had never been in the Bekkett Library's basement before.

"Wow! This is crazy! I've always been curious about meandering to the library's basement, but never saw a need," Gavin said to Marie.

"Really? I'm shocked you have never been down there. This is one of the few original buildings in town and -," Marie stopped when Gavin cut her off.

"And, it's been renovated over the years to maintain its historical value. Duh!" Gavin said hoping to sound a bit cultured in Bekkett history.

"Yes. That's obvious. What I was going to say prior to rudely being interrupted is that this building hasn't always been the library. It started as the town jail and courthouse. And *that's* why I'm surprised you have never been down there, Mr. My-Dad's-a-Cop," Marie said with a smile.

"What? It was a jail? I, too, am surprised I didn't know that," Gavin said. Inside, he was frustrated his dad never thought to bring him to this place. It fully represented his dad's career. Of course, this little secret was akin to much of how his dad lived his life, hiding so many secrets he didn't know what he could or could not share.

Marie continued with her history lesson. "Back in the gold rush days things could get a bit out of hand along Main Street. The city leaders built this place with a basement because they wanted the local drunks and lawbreakers to remain out of sight and earshot of those passing through. They were very concerned with appearances and creating a dark, damp basement that few wanted to return to seemed like a good punishment."

"Yeah, but it seems like a lot of work to dig a hole in the dry, hard ground and then pour solid walls back before the days of heavy machinery."

"Like I said. They were quite concerned with how things appeared. The work was worth the end result. Besides, it was built by those in trouble with the law. Their penance was to dig this basement and pour the concrete foundation and exterior walls. A future home for some of their closest friends!"

"So, when did the library take its place?" Gavin inquired.

"Well, it sat empty for a number of years in the early 1900's. Once the new city hall was built and the county took over housing inmates, this place became a storage locker. Not until the 1950s did a group of local women begin to organize the items down here. They threw out what had no value, sold some antique items, and then used the money to transform these vaults into a useable filing system of important information."

"So here we sit. In a dungeon researching information about another dungeon. This town's screwed up!" Gavin exclaimed.

September 14, 2013 – 2:00 PM

Six seemingly unproductive hours passed as quickly as the water outside was rising. When Gavin finally looked at his watch he was shocked at how much time had sped by.

"Hey, Marie. It's approaching two o'clock. I need a break. I'm hungry and I need to stretch my legs. Wanna go grab some lunch?"

"No thanks," Marie said without looking up from the papers she was examining. "I grabbed a protein bar before leaving my apartment. I have an extra for you if you don't want to leave."

"I appreciate the offer, but I'm not quite as dedicated as you in research. I need to go breathe in some fresh air. I'm going to drive home, change, grab some food, and then I'll meet you back here in about two hours. You sure you are okay down here? It's a bit creepy."

"You get used to this place. I've spent many hours down here. I like the seclusion it provides."

"Alright. I'll see you in two hours. Call sooner if you find anything of great importance."

"Will do. Take it easy out there," Marie called to Gavin as he ascended the stairs.

***

Gavin stepped outside and was quickly soaked. He ran to his car, jumped in the driver's seat, and closed his door to shield himself from the rain. He sat there for a moment listening to the hard drops of rain pound onto the metal roof of the car. The sound always brought back memories of his mom. The two of them would go on long, meaningless drives in the countryside during spring rainstorms. She said she loved the peace this weather brought. In retrospect, maybe the gray, drab storms were a reflection of her marriage. Gavin turned on the car and moved the dial on the temperature control closer to the red line. He turned on the defroster to clear the fog on the windshield that formed with the presence of Gavin's body heat and heavy breathing.

While waiting for a clear windshield to navigate from, Gavin turned his thoughts back toward his mom. Growing up with her was such comfort when his dad was often gone working late nights and evenings. They were an inseparable pair until Gavin got his driver's license. Like other teens, the milestone of gaining this rite of passage brought new-found freedoms. He began spending many evenings hanging out with friends thus leaving his mom alone at home while her men were out and about.

Gavin could not help but wonder if selfishly pursuing his own agendas while his mom sat home by herself led to her leaving without a trace. He logically knew it was not his fault. It was his dad, after all, who had been cheating on his mom. On both of them, really. If his dad had taken his job as a parent and husband more seriously Gavin may still have a mom around. On a day like this, he could call and banter with her about this crazy weather. But Gavin still wondered if he did something that pushed his mom out so completely. For years after she left, he would wait for her to call and provide an explanation and apology. Life carried on and so did Gavin, knowing his mom was never going to reach out as he always hoped.

The cruelty of his dad's betrayal and his mom's disappearance haunted Gavin. He stared blankly at the fog on the windshield as the defroster slowly cleared the glass. He took the window's cue and shook this memory from his brain. He had work to complete and errands to run and could not sit in his car wishing his mom were here again. Gavin then remembered he had left his phone in the car all morning and picked it up from the center cup holder. He unlocked the screen and saw his dad had texted him.

"At the EOC. Water's rising fast. Be safe."

It was little shock to have his dad announce his location. Gavin figured if his dad wasn't outside stirring up work among the police officers, he would be inside trying to direct it. He assumed his dad only sent the notification out of obligation or his swelling pride at being back at work. Gavin did not bother responding.

Driving south from the library, Gavin realized how much rain was accumulating. The drainpipes were taxed with water building up around the grates of the drain spouts. Gutters were full and lapping over the tops of the curbs. Even still, if he had not received so many weather alerts, he would have a hard time believing flooding was occurring just outside the town limits.

Slowly coasting down Sunset Street toward Bekkett's smallest bridge over Sand Creek, he looked ahead and wondered why traffic was at a standstill. He stopped a few feet behind the car in front of him and waited a moment. He moved his body side to side as it looked like no one was even in the car ahead of him. Gavin honked the horn and saw no movement or obscene hand gestures in response to the blaring noise.

He opened his door and got out of the car. The cover of trees above him kept the constant rainfall from drenching him. The problem was that the leaves would periodically fill with water and dump small cupsful to the ground below. Of course, Gavin timed his exit from his car to perfectly coordinate with one such spill. The water hit a bull's eye and went down the nape of his neck and soaked his back down to his waistline.

"Seriously?!" Gavin exclaimed out loud and looked up at the canopy of trees with ire.

He walked toward the bridge, pulled his shirt away from his body, and shook his upper torso. Not that he needed to get dry. He just hated the large puddle of water that had attacked him so ruthlessly. Small drops were more his style. As he got closer to the bridge, he could hear people hollering and gathering around the edge of the roadway. Some had cameras and phones taking pictures. He saw one female waving her arms above her head at someone further down the road. He followed her exaggerated waving to see what she was so emphatically trying to accomplish. He quickly realized the bridge was gone. *No way!* Gavin thought to himself.

He ran up to the crowd of people and looked down at the edge of the road. Jagged pieces of concrete and asphalt were all that remained of the once heavily traveled bridge. A chasm laid open with no hopes of crossing. The water was rushing at great speeds and had torn away the earth and foundation taking the bridge with it.

"What happened?" Gavin asked. No one said anything in response to his question. It was clearly evident what had happened. The crowd did not want to state the naively obvious.

"Dumb question," Gavin added. "Anyone know *how* it happened? I hope no one was on the bridge when it went."

"Thankfully, no one was hurt," a teenage boy said. "I was driving south on Sunset Street and saw something in the water, so I stopped. I looked closer and saw it was a roll off dumpster floating down the river! I couldn't believe it."

"Like one of those trash dumpsters at apartment buildings?" Gavin asked.

"No! It was huge. Probably twenty feet long and five feet tall. I just watched as it hit that big tree and knocked the tree over," the teen pointed to a fallen log leaning on the far bank of Sand Creek. "Then the dumpster kept floating along and slammed into the side of the bridge. A huge chunk of concrete broke off the bridge on the far side. It was so crazy. I grabbed my phone and took a video." The teen stopped talking and looked at his phone. He manipulated the screen and then handed it to Gavin. "You gotta see it to believe it."

Gavin took the phone and hit play. It was just as the kid described. A large yellow and green dumpster slammed against the bridge's center posts. Chunks of concrete were dripping off the side of the bridge like melting wax falling from a birthday candle. Due to his already noisy surroundings, Gavin could not hear all the sound in the video, except for the videographer's choice use of curse words.

Watching mesmerized, Gavin saw the dumpster slowly fill with rainwater as it tipped slightly toward the moving river water. The dumpster gulped up the water and, with startling suddenness, was swallowed by the river. As it went under the surface the concrete post holding the bridge also disappeared, apparently torn away by the weight of the water filled dumpster. Within seconds the bridge deteriorated on camera. Pieces of asphalt tried to cling to the banks on either side, but the erosion was swift and unable to support the weight of the bridge. With a final push from miscellaneous debris in the river, the bridge sank into the water below. The picture on the phone went blurry and Gavin heard frantic screaming.

"What happened?" Gavin asked handing the phone back to the teen.

"I looked up and saw a mini-van driving north, right toward the bridge. I dropped my phone and began yelling and waving my arms. Good thing she was driving so slowly. The van stopped within a few inches of going over."

Gavin looked across the expanse and saw a van stopped just as the teen said.

"Looks like you saved that family's life, kid," Gavin said. "Did anyone call the police?"

Another bystander in the crowd answered. "I did. Apparently, the other two bridges over Sand Creek are about to flood over and they're concerned the same thing may happen there. Unfortunately, they can't get here as Bekkett is essentially cut in two. South Bekkett and North Bekkett. They said since we're all here blocking the road, they will come here last. They have to close Third Street and West Eighth at the bridges first."

Gavin barely listened as he soaked in the enormity of what was happening. Bekkett, nor anyone in this region, had seen a storm of this size in centuries and he was stuck in the basement of a library researching folklore while he missed history in the making. He grabbed his phone from his back pocket and took a video. He then took still shots of the river and eroded banks on the other side. He could not help but wonder if Double K Ranch was underwater. And if it was, had Betty been able to escape or get rescued prior to its destruction?

Gavin asked a few others on his side of the creek if they had seen the bridge collapse, but apparently, the teen witness was the sole surveyor of the carnage as it happened.

"You've got a great story, kid. Here's my card. I work for the paper. When this all settles down, I'd love a copy of that video and a one-on-one interview with you."

Gavin walked away, but not before he heard the teen yell out, "It's already been uploaded to my social media accounts. Maybe you should call me!"

Gavin shook his head and kept walking toward his car. He backed up to the top of the hill and drove parallel to Sand Creek. From this elevated position, he could see parts of the creek through the houses and trees. Low lying lands were under water and, clearly, there would be millions of dollars in damage to the homes and businesses that would never be able to escape this quick rise in water.

Gavin drove east out of town and headed south on the newest road in town, Shelmer Drive. Sand Creek took a southern turn and the roadway had been rebuilt about twenty years ago with a much larger bridge to accommodate an area under the roadway Bekkett officials had created as a water sports entrance. He guessed the water park would most certainly be underwater, but the bridge was high and wide enough it should withstand the force of the water.

As Gavin turned south onto Shelmer Drive, he realized the entire town of Bekkett had also discovered only one route would remain open. There was a standstill of traffic as people were stopped along the bridge, wandering on foot to take a bird's eye view of Sand Creek as it had never been seen before.

Gavin had no patience for traffic, so he flipped a U-turn and had no choice but to head north back into town. He was not going to successfully navigate his way home. Instead, he stopped at the Loaf 'N Jug and grabbed a healthy snack of Skittles and beef jerky. Not sure when he'd get a chance for more food, Gavin also bought two Gatorade bottles, three bags of chips, pre-bagged donuts, and some cashews. He was clearly not a survivalist or even slightly prepared for this "end of the world" feeling. Nor was he the only one stocking up on convenience store snacks. The owner of the store was going to make a bit of extra cash tonight.

September 14, 2013 – 3:15 PM

Marie thrived in the quiet realm of this historical trove. It was her rightful place in this world. Tucked away in solace with thousands of documents to pore over. She had already ruled out 27 journals, books, and newspaper clippings. Due to her knowledge of the region, she usually had to read only a short clip to know if it was the time frame she was looking for or not. If she thought it might be a relevant time frame, she created a pile for a later, deeper review. If she knew it was not on topic or in the wrong era, she put those documents in a separate stack. She decided she could have Gavin dive deeper into the books she thought may have some info. It would be more efficient if she did the initial search and he did the more thorough research.

She was startled when Gavin entered the room and said, "Hey, you'll never believe what I saw!" Gavin saw Marie jump off the ground when he spoke. "Oh, sorry. I didn't mean to scare you. I figured you heard me open the door. You're really into this."

"It's okay," Marie said breathing heavily. "What did you see?"

"The bridge at Sunset Street is completely gone! I talked to some kid who saw a large dumpster slam into the bridge which caused it to collapse. It's totally crazy. You should take a break and go take a look. It's like the world's ending out there. Everyone's gawking along the creek and buying all the food from the Loaf 'N Jug."

"Really? Because it's raining? What's wrong with people?" Marie was a bit annoyed to be disturbed due to the absurdity of humanity.

"The news is calling this the 'Storm of the Century.' I believe it. I couldn't even get home. The town's cut off north and south. It's like our own Civil War. You gotta choose a side cuz there's no crossing once you pick one," Gavin said with sarcasm.

"It's not really like a war at all unless people are out there killing each other," Marie said curtly.

"Sorry. I should know better than to make historical references to the historian." *Sheesh.*

After a brief silence, Marie spoke up. "Sorry, I don't care about the world out there. I care about what we are doing. *We* are on a mission," Marie was sure to put her emphasis on including both of them. "I've got a stack of books you can dig into. They are written either during the time I'm interested in or in regard to that time frame. This stack over there," Marie pointed to the far corner, "is stuff that won't help us. Let's not waste any more time on those."

Gavin was about to speak up about his growing indifference to this research while a massive storm was tearing apart Bekkett. But, as he was about to speak, he remembered the journal entry he read earlier and couldn't so easily walk away from this mystery. "Okay. Am I just looking for the name Weston among those stacks of stuff? Or do I need to get really thorough in my reading?"

"I think starting with a search for Weston may be the easiest. I really don't know what else we should be searching for. Thanks, Gavin. This means a lot to me." Marie looked at Gavin, hoping to make eye contact and give him a reassuring smile. Despite her love for research, it was comforting to have someone else with her given how on edge she was at the topic of her search. Gavin did not return a look. Instead, he was carefully inspecting the wrapper of his donuts trying to determine how best to open the precious bundle without squishing the contents within. She watched as he finally clawed his way into the pack of powdered donuts and as he ate them one by one completely whole.

"Not going to savor each bite, hm?"

"Whaft?" Gavin made a muffled questioning noise. He continued to chew and swallow then looked at Marie with a large powdery grin. "Oh. I'm savoring them, alright! Want one?"

"Nope. I'm good. Thanks anyway."

September 14, 2013 – 3:45 PM

Taylor had spent most of his day in the basement. His friends had a love for entertainment and had five lounge chairs situated around an 80" high-definition LED screen. Blu-ray really was great when it was nearly life size. The booming base and THX-certified surround sound system kept him immersed in the theatrical performances he was watching.

Stretching from his lethargic state of being, Taylor went upstairs to get an update on the storm. The water had not risen much since the last time he had checked. Taylor thought it may have already hit its peak. Although, from his naked eye, the debris field around the fence post seemed to have increased.

Taylor sauntered to the smaller telescope and looked into the eyepiece again. He hadn't moved its position, so it was still focused on the same fence post he watched earlier. The magnification of the telescope made it clear more debris had lodged against the post. He took inventory of what would be there when the water subsided. After all, he would be the one tasked to clean it all up.

He saw several tires, some blue tarp, a lot of tree limbs, and what looked to be a dead animal or two. The storm caught even nature's creatures off guard. He moved the telescope and scanned the waterline to see if there were any other debris fields and saw none. Moving the sights back to the fence post, he pulled away from the telescope and took a step back. He would look again a bit later, if he felt like it. As he turned away from the window, recognition of what he had just seen sank in. His mind was not expecting anything out of the ordinary and it took a minute to process what it was he thought he had seen. He quickly turned and put his eye back to the telescope. In his hurry, he pushed the scope's view off where he needed it. He looked up and out the window and sighted the telescope toward the general area he wanted to see. He looked in the view finder and focused on the fence post again.

"Crap! That can't be! No way!" Taylor was yelling into the empty house. "No! No! No!"

As much as he did not want to believe what he was seeing, there was no denying a body was pushed into the debris. He first saw the green slipper, which he earlier had mistaken for underbrush. Upon closer examination, it was clearly a slipper attached to a foot which was attached to a leg. Next to the slippered foot, was an uncovered foot. Toes exposed. Wrinkles evident. *Were the wrinkles caused by the waterlogged state of the body or the age of the person to whom they belonged?* Taylor could not be certain. He could see nothing more than the two legs. The remainder of the body was obscured by a pile of grass and limbs.

Hoping the person was merely doing the backstroke he waited for movement. Taylor was silently pleading the legs would kick in the water and a smiling face would round the debris and swim toward the safety of the house. After a full ten minutes, the body only moved with the water's rise and fall. Whomever this was, they had succumbed to the water and the cold. Taylor ran to the phone and dialed 911.

"Nine-one-one. What's your emergency?" the call-taker said monotone.

"There's a dead body in the water near my house!" Taylor yelled into the phone.

The tone on the other end quickly filled with life, "Where are you?"

"I'm at 49102 Stagecoach Lane. You gotta help!"

"Is it a man or woman?"

"I can't tell. I was just looking through a telescope and saw some legs floating on the water. The top of the body is hidden behind a bunch of debris."

"Why do you think the person is dead?"

"I watched for about ten minutes and there was no movement. No way that person is alive."

"Please hold on a moment while I speak to the police and fire dispatcher."

"Okay, but you've gotta hurry!" Taylor said into a muted phone.

After a brief pause, the call-taker spoke again. "Sir. Are you safe? Our maps indicate your property is underwater."

"Me? Yeah, I'm safe. Wouldn't be talking to you if I were underwater. The house sits above the creek a ways, so there's no fear of getting wet in the house."

"That's good to hear. Do you know who the person in the water might be? Is there anyone missing from your house?"

"No. I'm here alone. I have no idea who it is. Are you on your way? I have a Jet Ski if you need to use it to get to the person."

"Sir, all the roads leading to your property are submerged. We have no way of getting out there. Furthermore, if the person is dead already, there is very little we can do. The county has already asked for help from other resources, but we are not able to help. We have too many other rescues of trapped and living people to take care of a possibly dead individual. If anything changes, please let us know."

"So that's it? You're not going to do anything? I just need to swim out there and get that person myself? Will you come help then – if I'm drowning?!" Taylor yelled into the phone.

"I understand you're upset. We are just not prepared to help the number of people that have called needing to be rescued. We have to focus on those that are still alive. Those we –"

Taylor had heard enough. He hung up the phone mid-sentence. Pissed at the insolence of those his taxpayer money employed, he threw his phone into the cushioned seat of the sofa.

"If you're not willing to help, I'll take care of this myself!" Taylor screamed at his phone. With that, he stomped into the kitchen and opened a drawer. He dug around for a minute looking for the key he knew was there among the junk. Finding the one marked 'JS' he turned and jogged out the front door and toward the barn.

Taylor slogged through the muddy field and walked up to the closed barn door. He slid open the latch on the door and began to push the hefty piece of solid wood. The ground was saturated, and Taylor slipped before he was able to dig his feet deep enough into the ground to reach a more solid footing. Pushing his legs against the ground, he used his arms to put pressure on the barn door to slide it open. Once he gained traction, the door slowly pushed away, and Taylor was met with the scent of grass clippings from the truck-sized lawn mower. He quickly savored the smell and stepped inside the barn. Ever since moving in, Taylor had not used the Jet Skis, so he wasn't quite sure how his hastily planned rescue would pan out.

He moved into the back corner of the barn and rounded the trailer. On its open bed were two Jet Skis tucked in for the winter. A lightweight blue tarp had been tossed over the Jet Skis to prevent dust buildup over the next five months of sedentary use. Taylor threw back the covering and only then began pondering his options. The water's edge was about 75 yards from the barn. He could not push the Jet Ski that distance, even over the water-soaked lawn outside. Of course, that wasn't even an option because there was no way to lift one of these off the trailer without help. There was only one solution. He was going to have to hitch the trailer to his truck and create his own boat ramp.

Taylor knew daylight was slipping closer to the western horizon. He ran back into the house and into his room. He grabbed his coat and his keys then ran back toward the front door. Only then did he realize he had tracked size twelve mud smears throughout the house. He would have to deal with that mess after he was done outside. Chances were good he'd be tracking more in later. He slipped on his coat, ran outside, and reached into his right pocket just as he got to the front door of his truck.

Backing into the barn was easy but aligning the hitch with the receiver was akin to threading a needle blindfolded. He was used to his boat and trailer where he could easily tell the bow of the boat was his target. This trailer had no visible center point. After six attempts, Taylor realized the gap between the two Jet Skis was as close to the center as he could get. Stopping at the first bump of the trailer, Taylor jumped out and was satisfied with the current alignment. Using his upper body strength, he pushed and jumped and kicked at the trailer until it dropped onto the hitch. Thankful he wouldn't need to hook up lights, he secured the chain from the trailer to his truck and drove out of the barn.

It wasn't until he was halfway toward the water's edge, he realized this plan was irresponsible and he was probably going to lose his truck in the muddy field. It would have to sit there paralyzed. But his only true concern was finding out whose legs were in the water. Taylor spun the wheel until the front of the truck pointed toward the house. Popping the gear into reverse, Taylor slowly backed up. Turning the wheel to re-direct the trailer seemed to be useless. It was relenting to the mud and once its course was set, he could not maneuver another direction. The wheels of the truck began spinning and the trailer dipped down, sinking further into the field. Taylor was still at least fifteen yards from the water and needed to get the trailer fully submerged if he hoped to get the Jet Skis loosened from the solid hold of the trailer.

"Come on! Come on! Go!" Taylor yelled as he hit the steering wheel with the palms of his hands.

Forgetting the stupidity of his plan, Taylor floored it. The trailer bounced out of its ruts and lurched toward the water much faster than Taylor anticipated. Yelling a string of curse words, Taylor gripped the steering wheel and made a quick turn. The back edge of the trailer dipped into the water and suddenly disappeared into what Taylor guessed was a hole. The other corner of the trailer protruded from the water and the Jet Skis seemed to be begging for action as the trailer pulled the truck backward.

Taylor switched gears to drive and stomped on the gas pedal until it touched the floorboard. The truck slid to the right, leveling out the trailer, but securing his truck into a tight relationship with the muddy ground. There was no more fight for the truck. Taylor threw it into park, jumped out, and stepped into a foot of cold, muddy water. Hopping onto the trailer, Taylor pulled a knife from his front pocket and cut the straps holding down the Jet Skis. Immediately, one pulled away and slid onto the water's surface. Before it could float away, he jumped onto its cushioned seat, landing sideways and on his stomach. A momentary loss of breath held him down. Taylor swung his legs around the back of the Jet Ski and he sat up. He inserted the key into the ignition and only then hoped there was fuel in the tank. The Jet Ski sputtered to life and Taylor let out a joyous holler.

He hadn't driven one of these watercrafts since high school, but it was much like riding a bike. Once he got the hang of it, he quickly turned toward the debris field. Taylor slowed to a crawl and had to adjust his heading to compensate for the current pulling him away from his target. After a few minutes, he was able to reach the top of the fence post. He hung onto the post for a moment and tried to stand up and look over the branches but could not see the legs. Afraid of getting a limb or the fence rails stuck under the Jet Ski, he needed to plan his route carefully. Since he had not grabbed a life vest, he had to be more cautious than he normally would care about.

Watching the current and the ripples on the water's surface, Taylor decided to jet around the pile with a fifteen-foot arc. He would head into the current and allow it to guide him back toward the gathering logs. The plan worked more perfectly than he could have hoped for. He was pushed into a large tree trunk and able to stop without too much wobbling or pulling away from the mystery legs.

Taylor stood up and looked toward the area where the torso would have been based on his last sighting of the legs from the telescope. At first, he could not see a body. He quickly looked side to side and wondered if this entire scene was his twisted imagination. Taylor bounced up and down, causing the Jet Ski to be carried by the current a few feet. He investigated the muddy water again hunting for the body. "Holy . . ." Taylor exclaimed. This was repeated four more times.

The legs were mere stumps. He could see one perfectly manicured foot and followed it to the knee. Just below where the knee should have been, were jagged pieces of flesh. The other mangled leg lay parallel to the first. This one had more flesh and was not removed from the body until its pelvis area. A scrap of clothing twisted around both legs and hung onto them like cling wrap keeping leftover dinner from spilling off the plate.

Taylor threw up.

He reached into his coat and took a picture using his phone. He thought about grabbing the pieces of flesh and bringing them back to dry land but realized he was never going to stomach doing that. Besides, the 911 dispatcher had a point. What would they do with a dead body in this weather anyway?

Taylor threw up again.

A sudden chill crept over Taylor. It was the realization the flesh was not merely separated by a freak accident. It looked more like an animal devoured the body. Taylor quickly glanced around him. The hair was beginning to stand up on the back of his head and he couldn't help but wonder if the water had unleashed some Lochness-type monster. He needed to get back to land.

Taylor pushed the throttle on the watercraft and beached his transportation in the field. Standing on shaky knees, Taylor pulled his phone from his pocket. He opened the pictures and still could not believe what he had seen. Sliding through the pictures, he was glad to have this evidence. Without it, there was no chance of anyone in town believing this tale of gruesome discovery.

While still gawking at his phone, Taylor saw movement out of his periphery of what looked like a bear walking past the barn. Fear and curiosity pulled at Taylor's ability to listen to reason. He was anxious to get a closer look. He had not seen any bears around this area and wondered where it had been hiding. It would have had to have been close by to be on his property now. He was stuck on an island, so the bear didn't wander here from the mountains overnight. He could not help but wonder if it was responsible for the sight he had just seen in the water.

As he stood still, the animal walked out of his view, on the far side of the house. Taylor decided to round the house from the opposite direction and face it head-on rather than chase it from behind. He sloshed through the muddy field toward the corner of the house. Although he would never admit to being afraid, he was a bit concerned about the thought of looking a bear dead in its eyes. Taylor pressed himself against the siding of the house and decided to take a quick glance around the corner. He squatted down and slowly looked around the edge of the house. As soon as his right eye rounded the corner, he could see the brown fur of the animal. It appeared to be sitting down, its back to Taylor. Using one eye to look did not provide the clarity he wanted so Taylor moved until his entire head was exposed. From this vantage point, both eyes were peering at the back of a peculiar animal. It had the fur of a bear, but the body type of a gorilla or ape, judging by the way it was sitting on the ground.

Taylor slowly stood up to give rest to his weary hamstrings. Squatting while twisting one's body around the corner of the house was not a comfortable pose to hold for long. Pulling his cell phone from his pocket, he lifted it to eye level and held the shutter button down. His phone took a burst of 10 rapid photos. But the speed of the camera's shutter was no match for the swiftness of the creature in front of him. He had not silenced his phone and when he took the picture, the phone's manipulated audio sound of a camera click sounded much louder in the silence of this moment.

The bear also heard the sound. Before he could even release the phone's button to stop taking photos, the bear had turned its head. Only then did Taylor realize this was no bear. This was no gorilla or ape. This was a creature like none he'd ever witnessed. Its eyes, if it had any, were buried deep in a recessed forehead covered with matted fur. A nose sat twisted on its face and as it turned it inhaled deeply. Time slowed for Taylor, whether by fear or fate, and he was able to see minute details of this thing in front of him. As the creature inhaled, bits of fur from around the nostrils were pulled into the holes, flapping in the significant breeze its inhaling brought. The exhale came from a gaping hole under the nose which was surrounded by sharp brownish white teeth. Each tooth was an incisor. Sharp and clearly able to devour the toughest of meats with the ease of a new chainsaw through a small branch.

Taylor had lowered his phone slightly but hung on to it out of sheer fear of what he was facing. His left hand clutched the phone and his thumb pressed the shudder, snapping another series of pictures. The beast, the best word for what stood before him now, had turned its body and stood. This thing had more joints than a normal animal and its legs seemed to unfold four times as it stood to an elevated height of more than eight feet. Taylor was filled with awe and wonder and the knowledge he may not live to tell others of this moment.

The beast leaned forward and rested on its arms. It continued to inhale deeply, and its cavernous eyes fixated on Taylor as he slowly swiped his finger over the screen of his phone. With a few short, memorized movements, he sent his photos to the only person in town who just might believe this craziness. Gavin was a good reporter and would jump at the chance to investigate this thing.

Taylor took one step back and pushed record on the video on his phone. He then tossed his phone to the ground, out of sight of this creature. If it killed him, he wanted the police to at least find his phone and the evidence of his demise. The creature looked down and arched its back while it put the full weight of its body on its feet and hands. From this angle, it could almost be mistaken for an extremely large dog merely stretching after a contented nap.

With the suddenness of a rubber band being shot from one's hand, the beast lunged forward. Without a chance of fleeing, Taylor eyed the claws of the creature which appeared from the palms of its hands. There would be no victory for Taylor. The beast pounced, launching three feet into the air. It landed on top of Taylor with enough force to completely knock the wind out of his lungs. As Taylor gasped for breath, the beast paused and looked into his open mouth. Taylor sucked in bits and pieces of air, but not enough to produce any relief from the crushing he felt on his chest. As Taylor continued to struggle for air the beast merely eyed him with curiosity. Unbeknownst to its prey, the beast was waiting for a scream - its joyous request to devour its meal. This thing it had captured made no noise, enraging the beast. It moved within an inch of Taylor's face and opened its mouth. Leaning back, it let out a roar so deafening Taylor was sure he would lose all hearing.

The beast stopped, sat up then began swinging its arms like a pendulum over Taylor's belly. Each swipe of the arm eviscerated his flesh, exposing blood and internal organs. The beast stood over Taylor's crippled form and took another deep breath. It bowed down toward Taylor's body and licked the blood from his wounds. The pain was so intense, Taylor was begging for death. As if knowing Taylor's thoughts, the creature grasped Taylor's neck and began to apply pressure. Its claws were digging into Taylor's neck and blood began spurting into the waiting face of the beast. Its open mouth lapped up the flying blood. Without notice, the other arm of the beast swung down on Taylor's head, causing a fatal blow. The beast knew its meal could not flee and it sat down beside the lifeless body and slowly pulled the flesh off its body as if the beast were snacking on string cheese. Its appetite would be satiated for a long while.

September 14, 2013 – 6:50 PM

Gavin replayed the image in his mind. Occasionally he would utter his disbelief out loud. "How could a huge metal dumpster float down a river and then cause the collapse of a bridge?" Marie listened half-heartedly but was clearly much more into her research than the elements raining down on her hometown. She was on a mission and Gavin could not fault her for seeking the truth so desperately. This had been a years-long journey for Marie, and she was standing at the edge of discovery. He couldn't help but be swept into this journey with her.

"Marie, it's nearly seven o'clock and, truth be told, I'm getting hungry. It turns out candy, chips, and flavored water only sustain my hunger for so long," Gavin said.

"If you're asking if I want to take a meal break, the answer is no. I don't have much of an appetite when I research. Especially when I'm this close to my discovery. I know you're anxious to get some fresh air, so don't feel bad if you need to leave for a bit. You don't have to come back, either. But this will go much more quickly if you're able to lend a hand," Marie said not really wanting Gavin to leave for the night. The company, quiet as it was, was good.

"I'm just going to run up the street to Lefty's Pub. I'll get some food, check my messages, and bring something back for you. They have killer salads. What's your dressing of choice, Marie?"

"Blue Cheese. And a sweet tea. Thanks, Gavin," Marie said.

"You got it. I'll be back in an hour or so."

As soon as Gavin exited the building, a series of alert tones and vibrating sequences brought his phone to life. The basement swallowed his phone's ability to connect with the world. It was a black hole of historical documents. Eyeing the screen, he could see he had missed three phone calls from his dad and a text message from Taylor. Gavin was alarmed that his father would call him three times. Something must be askew for his dad to try and reach him so repetitively. Since his dad was working the EOC, maybe he was calling to provide Gavin an inside scoop. Of course, in this small town, he was more likely to get a great scoop from the ice cream shop than anyone else in this town.

Ignoring the calls from his dad, Gavin thumbed over the text from his friend. A black screen with a spinning circle prompted Gavin to be patient. Taylor had obviously sent a large file which was taking its sweet time downloading. The storm was interfering with the cellular waves and the status of the file didn't budge. It was clearly going to take a while. Knowing his dad was not going anywhere soon, Gavin closed the text from Taylor and checked the AP wire for news updates on this incredible storm. Reports were coming in from all along the front range region of mass flooding, power outages, and residents stuck in houses bordering the once dry Sand Creek. Local police departments were asking for aid from other agencies to assist with traffic control and to reduce the threat of looters. The fire department had been performing technical rescues in Bekkett and other towns that seemed to have fared much worse. Gavin was swept up in the stories as he walked into Lefty's Pub and sat at the bar.

He looked up only to order a drink and some food and immediately got immersed in the stories from across the region. The sheer amount of water and the incredible torrents of rain left people stranded or in serious danger for miles in all directions. The flooding was expanding beyond the front range. As the waterways headed east, so did the destructive deluge. Any community that sat along the banks of rivers fed by a mountain stream was at risk of being washed away. The inches of rain that fell in such a short amount of time had been completely unpredicted to this extent. Communities were caught off guard until it was too late to safely gather property and flee. The National Guard sent helicopters to mountain regions where residents had become trapped in the solitude once so accepting of their stay. Nature was kicking them out.

It wasn't until Gavin was heading back to the library with Marie's food and drink order that he remembered his dad had called. Gavin dialed his dad and waited for three rings before his dad's familiar voice answered, "Gavin? You okay? I've tried calling you at least three times this afternoon. Where have you been?"

"Sorry, dad. I didn't mean to worry you. I've been out and about a bit. I'm stuck on the north side of Bekkett. Looks like the city's cut in half. I've spent the rest of my time in the basement of the library."

"The old jail? What on earth are you doing down there? It's nothing but historical documents and old lady's mindless gossip from the days when the Gazette had nothing better to print than the social gatherings of everyone in town. Do you know, I once read an article about the Mayor's wife hosting a party for her extended family that arrived in town from North Carolina? They even wrote incredible journalism about their meal and family lineage." The sarcasm in his voice was more than evident. "I'm glad your work at the Gazette has been of far more interest to this community!"

"Well, thanks for the compliment. Glad I can write better than a gossip column. It's what I've aspired to accomplish," Gavin matched his dad's sarcasm. "So, dad, did you call merely to check up on me? Or was there something else on your mind?"

"I really just wanted to make sure you were okay. This storm is like nothing I've ever witnessed before. They're calling it the 500-year flood. But I'm guessing you've heard that by now."

"Yeah, just read that a bit ago. Since you're in the EOC and in the know, why don't you tell me what the papers haven't heard yet? Is the city about to be flooded and swept away? Will

Bekkett's glorious dynasty wash away with the current?" Gavin said with a chuckle.

"You'd like that, wouldn't you? Fact is, there's not much we know that the reporters don't also know. The police scanner is accessible to the public's ear, and you know they've been glued to the radios as we dispatch officers and deputies all over the county. Bekkett's own police force has been mainly doing evacuations. That and becoming glorified road workers as they close roads and then watch as people ignore the cones. There's little we can do to stop all the looky-loos."

"Yeah, I saw a bit of that earlier at the Sunset Street bridge. They're crazy dad. It's what kept you employed for so many years. It's why you still have work to do, even in retirement," Gavin said with irritation.

Ignoring Gavin's tone, Tom replied, "No shortage of dumb around here, Gavin. Listen, I don't want to alarm you unnecessarily, but we've had unconfirmed reports that the Double K Ranch was taken over."

"What do you mean, dad? The National Guard setting up camp there or something?"

"No, son. It was swallowed by water. No one's heard from Betty. That's why I was calling you. I know you and Marie were doing some research there yesterday."

"How do you know? I haven't told anyone."

"Gavin. I'm retired. Not a moron. You called your buddy with the sheriff's department about Marie flipping her car in a ditch over there. I'm in the know. I'm just glad you're okay."

"Wow. Even as an adult, I can't hide anything from you, can I?" Gavin asked incredulously.

"I'm not trying to pry, Gavin. We all know what prying eyes can see." Even as Tom spoke these words, he knew he should have kept them to himself. He should not be placing blame on Gavin for his own transgressions. If Gavin had not discovered the affair, someone else eventually would have.

Tom continued, hoping his words didn't sink in. "I just care about you."

"Yeah, whatever. Spying on me doesn't really say 'I love you, kid.' It's a bit more freaky than that dad. I'm surprised you didn't know I was in the library basement all afternoon too."

"Hey . . ." Tom didn't have any words and let the phone fall silent.

"Listen, dad. I'm okay. I get it. You don't want anything to happen to me. I'm stuck inside anyway. No way I'm getting swept away by any flooding tonight. I've got Marie's food and it's getting cold, so I'm gonna go. I'm in the basement, so I'll be out of reach until I ascend from the trenches again." Gavin added, a bit reluctantly, "Thanks for checking on me." Before he could get an answer, Gavin hung up and descended into the library basement. This time he stomped down the steps so Marie wouldn't jump in fear when he first spoke.

"I'm so glad you're back, Gavin!" Marie jumped up with a book in her hand. "I found a lot of material about this guy Weston! You wanna hear?"

"I do. But point me in the correct direction. You need to eat. I'll read what you've found while you take a break." Gavin offered no room for debate, as he took the book from Marie's hand and replaced it with a salad and fork. "And here's your sweet tea," Gavin added, setting it on the table next to Marie.

**

Gavin read, sometimes aloud, the information Marie had found about Weston. It seemed he was the real founder of this desolate region, not the Bekkett's. Somehow, Gavin was not sure just yet, the Bekkett's had superseded Weston in fame and infamy into this region's growth. From what he had read so far, he learned Weston had traveled to this region with a group of slaves he had acquired from his time in southern Florida. Apparently, Weston was an intelligent man who knew a difference of thought on slave ownership was brewing and he needed to leave the southern states before his property was rudely taken from him.

His journey ended in Bekkett where he retained his wealth but only half his slaves. Many had died along the difficult trek west. Weston's business acumen kept him alive even though he was a foreigner among the natives who thrived in the region. His charming character allowed him to barter back and forth and build positive relationships with the region's inhabitants. Gavin flipped through a few more journals Marie had set aside. They were accounts of Weston's wealth and odd character that both drew people into his world and kept them at bay. It seemed only those Weston deemed worthy were ever allowed to get close to him. Gavin read on while Marie took a much-needed break.

"Several documents have mentioned Lady Okayo Guerday. Who the heck is she? She seems to be described as a servant of Weston's, but she also seems to have more authority in his realm than a slave or servant would typically have," Gavin said to Marie.

"I saw the name once. You say you've seen it several times? Where?" Marie asked as she moved to Gavin's side to look at the same documents he was reading.

"Here and here. And in that book to your right." Gavin pointed to a small red leather-bound journal.

"Do you think she was from Louisiana? The name sounds Cajun. Maybe on his journey this way he met up with her," Gavin guessed.

"I suppose that's a possibility. But, why?" Marie asked. "Anyway, I'm not sure it really even makes a difference. Weston is the guy I'm most curious about. Now, the real question, is how does he connect with the beast? What can we learn here that ties into what the journals have told us?"

"Are you serious? Lady Okayo has to be our Lord of the Rain, Marie!" Gavin exclaimed. "It makes so much more sense now that we can piece it all together."

"Oh my gosh!" Marie groaned loudly. "How could I be so dumb? I've read so many things I completely forgot about the old lady from the journals in my apartment. This is the very reason I need help. The words blend together and having a second set of eyes brings clarity!"

"I'm here for ya," Gavin said with a smile.

"Thank you, thank you, thank you!" Marie gushed. "It's all coming together. I'm sure the answers are in these stacks of pages. Are you going to stick around and help me?" Marie asked.

"I just had my reprieve, so I guess I'm here to complete the rest of my prison sentence. It's an appropriate location after all," Gavin said.

September 14, 2013 – 10:00 PM

Tom & Gregg stood in the corner of the EOC silently watching and listening to the buzz of the room. Town personnel crowded into the room attempting to assuage the fears of Bekkett's citizens. The room was full of dozens of people who selflessly left their homes and families to do whatever they could to minimize damage to their town. The effort from those in the EOC was echoed by the many personnel in the storm setting up barricades, responding to emergencies, and directing people away from danger.

Gregg knew of at least two employees whose homes were not only evacuated but were also in the path of the water's raging fury. Memories were going to be lost as they were washed away to never be seen again. Despite their devastation, it was awe-inspiring to see their dedication. He could only assume there were others he didn't know about in the same boat. Gregg silently laughed at his unintended pun. It was dumb humor that would keep him from emotionally breaking down.

"Gregg," Tom verbally nudged. "Gregg, you there? Earth to Gregg."

"Sorry. I was just watching in amazement at what we've got going in here," Gregg replied.

"Yep. Nothing short of self-sacrifice. Frank over there," Tom said pointing, "was told about an hour ago that his mom's house flooded. She's safe on the upper level but trapped. He's a rock."

"Geez. I hadn't heard about Frank. I was just thinking of what Dave must be going through. His home, heck his entire neighborhood, took the brunt of the river's new warpath. Reports are sketchy, but that's where the fire department had to do most of their water rescues."

"It's incredible. Who would have ever thought the Bekkett Fire Department would pair up with the Coast Guard in our land-locked community to complete life-threatening water rescues?" Gregg's words trailed off at the sheer enormity of what was happening.

Tom closed the silence and asked, "Hey, are you listening to these phone calls, Gregg? There has to be at least five reports of missing people and another thirty of missing pets."

"That's bound to happen. I'm not too surprised," Gregg replied. "It would make sense the sudden amount of water has cut off both humans and their pets from one another."

"Something doesn't sound right, though. Some reports are from people who couldn't evacuate. You know, those who had to shelter in their homes, but are trapped. I've heard several tell our dispatchers that one moment their pet was wandering the yard and the next moment, after an unearthly scream, their pets were gone."

"Tom. You know as well as I that turmoil like this freaks people out. They see things. They hear things. They mess up their facts. It's typical behavior."

"Normally, I would agree, Gregg. But the bit about the screaming has been consistent. I might not even give it much thought over pets that may tend to wander and get swept away. But there are similar reports involving people. They have just vanished. I've got that creepy sixth sense feeling. I can't think of a time it steered me wrong. Something's not right out there," Tom concluded his thoughts while pointing to the exterior window and into the darkness.

As Tom finished speaking, he decided not to wait for a reply. A thought crossed his mind and he turned from Gregg's side and walked to the call taker's station. He picked up a stack of reports of the pets and people reported missing. Flipping through the data, he saw one consistency. The reports coming in were all along the waterway.

Tom took the reports to the town mapping desk. "Hey, Nora. Can you generate a map for me? I need these locations pinpointed on the map with a corresponding time stamp."

"Tom. You know I love you, but in case you haven't noticed, we're mapping the river's movement and every point where it's breached its banks. Your little project is going to have to wait. I'm really sorry."

Tom was about to protest but knew Nora was correct. He could not supersede Nora's work at saving lives with only his hunch. "You're right. Sorry to bother you. Can you tell me where I can find a large map of the town? I'll use it to do this project myself."

Nora pointed toward the opposite side of the room and said, "There through the back door of the EOC, take a right and you will see there's a stack of maps on the printer in the Tech Room. Help yourself."

"Thanks. And keep up the good work!" Tom said as he briskly walked toward the Tech Room.

September 14, 2013 – 11:00 PM

Steve was tired. Physically, emotionally, and spiritually. Running the Red Cross shelter had drained every ounce of his psyche. He was grateful for the outpouring of support from the community, the Red Cross, his congregation, and the government. But he still needed a break. Heading to his office, he kept the lights off. He closed the door behind him and saw only the red glow of the clock that faintly displayed the late hour. The day had flown by. It seems just a few minutes ago he had received the first alert. In reality, it was 21 hours ago.

Steve sat in the recliner in his office. On a typical day, these chairs were reserved for counseling sessions. He leaned back and took a few deep breaths and let his mind travel to the past. His tour in Iraq seemed so insignificant now in comparison to the devastation he witnessed today. Of course, he saw very little action during his two months overseas. During a so-called routine patrol, his convoy had been ambushed by insurgents. At some point in the gunfight, the driver of his Humvee had to take evasive maneuvers to avoid running over their own troops. As the vehicle dropped off the side of the road, an IED exploded just under the passenger compartment. The protective measures on the Humvee saved Steve's life. Unfortunately, the blast was still severe enough to remove his right foot.

Steve was rushed to the on-scene medics and eventually airlifted to a hospital in Germany. He spent several months recovering from his wound. While walking the halls of the medical ward with his physical therapist, Steve recognized his missing foot was inconsequential when compared to the other men and women who had suffered so much worse. Steve's negative outlook quickly shifted to joy and peace when he realized how lucky he really was.

Reflecting on that time in his life, Steve let out a soft chuckle. Had that day never occurred in Iraq, he wouldn't be the lead pastor of a thriving church today. He still couldn't fully understand God's design in this world. There were no logical answers to loss and devastation. During his recovery and his first few months stateside, Steve found the platitudes of so many people trite and downright offensive. If it weren't for his renewed faith in God while in Germany, he may have allowed those words to drive him toward anger. Instead, he allowed the experience to move him toward becoming the kind of pastor who was able to care for the lost and hurting people in this world. Whether their hurt be physical pain or emotional loss, Steve knew more than most people that words of encouragement had little value toward actual healing. It was his heartfelt mission to meet people in their pain, and his ability to physically relate to loss, that allowed his ministry to thrive.

Steve took a few minutes to sit in silence and whisper what little words of prayer he could. What, really, could he even pray? Over the course of the day, so many people had told him stories that far exceeded any pain he ever experienced. Most were lucky just to get out of their homes before the flood surge swept away their lives. There were countless stories pouring in of parents who had less than five minutes to wake up, dress, rouse their children, and flee before their homes were washed away. So many memories were now lost in the flood.

Factual news reports were minimal in the wake of such destruction. Cloud cover kept aerial views from occurring and washed away bridges kept people out or in, depending on which side of the bridge people were. In light of not knowing more facts, he took to heart the stories being shared in the church gymnasium. There were so many stories of devastation and fear being shared by those who had fled or been rescued. The few who came to the church for food and shelter spoke of a loss which was generally seen only on television. The type of destruction you watched while silently thanking God it was happening somewhere else. Unfortunately, today, it was happening here. Those that escaped damage were now saying a simple prayer of thanks for their protection.

Forty minutes into a much-needed nap, Steve's eyes shot open. Something had startled him awake. He sat in silence trying to get his mind to replay what it was that alarmed him from his slumber. Then it hit him. It was a scream. An ungodly, otherworldly guttural scream. Too unnatural to have come from this realm.

The spirit of Loa had been disturbed. The Bekkett Beast was roaming. Steve knew in his soul this to be true. He left his chair and went straight to his knees. *God, protect us. Kill the beast. Do not allow it to harm this community. We've experienced too much pain already.* As if defying Steve's spiritual task, another scream arose from the silence. Steve feared it would take much more than prayer to destroy the beast.

***

It had taken Tom an hour to find the map, gather some pins, get a workspace, and begin mapping the disappearances. From what information he gleaned from the call takers, he was able to pinpoint thirteen missing pet and people reports from five-thirty this morning until nine o'clock tonight.

He took a step back from the map. Just as he suspected, the reports were rolling into town, from west to east. The first was just east of Double K Ranch. The most recent was only one-half mile outside of Bekkett's city limits. From all appearances, the missing were flowing with the water. Logically, it made sense. But logic was not at play tonight.

He had no way to theorize what this discovery meant or if anyone would even care. The simple truth was obvious. As the water moved east, the level rose, the current increased, and it was likely that people and pets were merely swept away. It was the most plausible explanation. But something kept eating away at Tom. Something was not sensible about any of this. However, until he had a solid theory to provide to the Town Manager, he was not going to risk sounding the fool and promptly being asked to leave.

Tom realized he had only one option. He needed to call Gavin. He could sound a fool to Gavin and not lose any status. And, by chance, if Gavin had any belief in the story, he would be one to seek out the truth. Discovering the truth among the lies was something Gavin did all too well. His need for truth and enjoyment of digging into the unknown is what made him a good reporter. Tom reluctantly picked up his phone to make the call. This was going to become Gavin's biggest story ever or what drove him further from his dad.

Tom heard three rings and then, "Hi. This is Gavin. Can't take your call."

"Gavin. I really need to talk to you. I've . . . discovered something. It's too weird to leave a message. It's urgent you call me back." Tom hung up and hoped it wouldn't be long for Gavin to return his call.

September 15, 2013 – 1:00 AM

Gavin was tired. He had only fitful bits of sleep in the last few days and his eyes were unable to keep the pull of gravity from winning. He was the first of the two to speak in what felt like hours. "Marie, I think we have hit a dead end. Aside from the property deed with Weston's name on it, we have not found much new information down here. And even that bit of info tells us little of any value."

Marie was not quite ready to leave. "I would really like a more definitive answer as to what that deed was for. Do you think it's possible he owned all the land prior to the Bekkett's? Maybe he sold it to them and left."

"I would agree except there was no amount listed on the transaction and the signature scribbles looked eerily similar. Maybe your coveted Bekkett family killed Weston, stole his land via a forged deed, and erased any memory of him or his legacy. Have you considered that Marie?"

"No, I can't say that I have. Although, it seems the most legitimate reason for their secrecy that I could think of. Hmm. If they killed a man and stole his land, then creating a story of a scary creature would have far more credence. To cover up their murderous deceptions, they simply come up with a story so unbelievable it may actually work at driving others away from their land."

"Sounds like you've solved the problem, here, Marie. The Bekkett's were not good people, were jealous of another man's success, killed him, stole his land, and created a lie."

"I don't buy it, Gavin. I just can't believe we've spent this much time down here and that is the best theory we have. And that theory of yours still negates the reality of the beast. I still think there's more than you are willing to accept," Marie said exasperated. She was tired and losing hope of finding any answers. Her disappointment in how this day was turning out was beginning to show. When she got up so many hours earlier, she really thought she would be lying awake now because of her discovery. Not because she was still clueless.

"I think we need a break. You know how easy it can become to miss something important as all the pages begin to blend into one," Gavin said.

"You may be right, Gavin," Marie replied. "If we go outside for a bit, get some fresh air, then come back reenergized, maybe we will finally find the clues we need to figure out Weston, Lady Okayo, the Bekkett's and the beast. There has to be more that we have missed."

Gavin stood up and stretched. "You really won't believe the devastation the water has caused out there. I know you want to find the answer to one of Bekkett's greatest historical mysteries, but you are about to have your eyes opened to history in the making," Gavin said reassuringly.

"They are really calling it a five-hundred-year storm?" Marie asked. After Gavin spoke with his dad, he passed on that piece of news to Marie hoping it would entice her out of the basement. It hadn't worked then, but it was gaining steam now.

"Yep. That means you have an opportunity to document history as it is made. Maybe returning to Bekkett was not about a fairy tale search as much as it will be about this moment in time. Right here. Right now," Gavin said.

"Okay," Marie replied. "Let's be a part of history." Marie stood, stretched her tired legs and climbed the stairs into the cloudy, starless night.

***

Gavin drove Marie around town, starting at the Sunset Street bridge collapse. He needed her to see the devastation of this storm first-hand. He repetitively relayed to her what he had seen over the last few hours. Now, he wanted her to finally understand the reality of what they were experiencing.

"You tell a pretty good story, Gavin," Marie quipped. "I pictured this almost exactly as you so continuously described it." Marie let out a small laugh as she made fun of Gavin relentlessly telling the same story.

"I guess it's why I have a job at the paper. Maybe I need to start a podcast too. Then, I can tell the story once and annoy you as I replay the podcast non-stop," Gavin jested in return.

After leaving the bridge, they drove toward Twin Peaks Golf Course on the west side of town. Gavin hoped he could skirt around the west side of town and then head south. They were unprepared for what they witnessed. The National Guard was on post with roadblock signs keeping them from driving any further west.

"What the..." Marie's voice trailed off. She had a hard time comprehending seeing military personnel in her sleepy town. It felt too much like a scene out of Hollywood.

"Hard to imagine having the National Guard here, huh," Gavin said.

"And the Coast Guard," Marie replied. Then she lifted her hand and pointed to a boat bobbing up and down in the water just beyond the roadblock with its emblem blazoned on the side of the boat.

"Unbelievable," was all Gavin could muster in response.

The two got out of the car and walked toward the roadblock. Gavin donned his identification card that read "Reporter" in bold black letters. Usually, it allowed him the opportunity to move beyond crime scene tape and get exclusive reports. But this was not the local police force. The men and women posted here had a serious task and they may not care that he was a reporter.

"Hi!" Gavin called out to the first uniformed guard member. "I'm with the local paper, The Bekkett Gazette. I was hoping I may be able to get a closer view with my photographer," Gavin added as he pointed toward Marie. She incoherently waved at the guard member.

The guard member scrutinized his ID and then replied, "Go ahead. You won't get too far anyway. The water's edge is just beyond our checkpoint here. Just don't be stupid and try to wade through the water. There are reports of very large sinkholes where roadways have simply collapsed under the weight of the water. We do not need to be making a night rescue for the two of you."

"No worries," Gavin said. "I like to be around after the fact to actually report what I see." Then he added, "Thank you for your service." The guard member nodded in response and stepped aside slightly for Gavin and Marie to walk by on dry ground.

It was hard to recognize the destruction before them. The night was dark and no lights were illuminated. The power lines were inoperable sending western Bekkett into oblivion. Gavin suddenly turned and ran toward his car. "Wait here, Marie!" he yelled over his shoulder.

A few minutes later Gavin returned with what appeared to be a set of binoculars. "Here," Gavin said to Marie as he handed the device to her. "These are night vision sights. You'll be able to get a better grasp of what is out there."

Marie pressed the device to her forehead and adjusted her eyes. "This can't be," Marie whispered. "Everything is gone. I only see water." She continued to scan from side to side. "Unreal. The golf course is completely underwater. That doesn't even matter when you see only the second-floor windows and roofs of the nearby houses. Those people have lost everything!"

Marie pulled the night vision from her face and handed them to Gavin. She put her hand on his shoulder and pointed to their left. "Look over there. That neighborhood is nearly submerged," Marie said.

"My God," Gavin muttered. "I hope everyone got out." He silently prayed to the name he had just invoked.

They took turns using the night vision to take in the sights in front of them. The horizon they previously knew as well-manicured golf greens and sand traps had been obliviated. The neighborhood to the south of the golf course was the scene from an apocalyptic movie. The top of a swing set bobbed on the surface of the water. Wading pools were sucked from backyards by the current that now anchored them against chimneys and trees.

Gavin turned to Marie, "You realize the river is south of here, and the current is running from the north. That means the water came from... well, I don't know where. Sand Creek is not to the north. Nothing is. Where did this water come from?"

Marie turned and walked back toward the female guard member. "Hey, you have sec?"

"I'm not going anywhere," she replied. "What's up?"

"What happened? Sand Creek is that way," Marie said as she pointed south. "But the water is flowing from over there," this time pointing toward the north.

"Reports are sketchy still. We had a few helicopter rescues from the mountains, but other than that, no flights are able to get over this region. It's just too dangerous. From what we can gather, Dry Creek merged with Peaceful Waters River and essentially created an entirely new waterway. The rush of water forged new paths. With all the rain, the grounds were saturated, and the water had nowhere to go but downhill. Straight toward your town. I'm sorry," the woman stated.

"It's incomprehensible," Marie said quietly.

Gavin then asked, "What's with the Coast Guard boat over there?"

"They came up from Denver. Apparently, even in land-locked Colorado, the Coast Guard has an auxiliary unit. They, along with other swift water rescue groups, were called up here to help evacuate that neighborhood," the woman explained.

"The Coast Guard in Bekkett," Gavin wondered out loud. "Wow."

"You should have seen them at work! The neighborhood you were just looking at trapped its residents very quickly. Those not fortunate enough to escape before the flood were forced to retreat to their second floor. The water lapped up everything below that. The Coast Guard, your local fire department, animal control officers, along with other swift water rescue groups made about ten trips into the neighborhood to rescue people and pets."

"If I were not standing here looking at this and personally hearing you tell me this," Gavin paused and then continued, "I don't know if I would believe it."

"I agree," Marie added. She turned to Gavin silently reminding him they had other projects to work on. Then she turned to the guard and said, "Thank you for your service. Please stay safe."

Gavin and Marie walked back to Gavin's car and sat down inside. They were silently taking in the sights of what they had just witnessed.

"I'm so glad you got me out of that basement," Marie said as she looked at Gavin. "I can't believe I was about to miss the enormity of this storm."

"There's really no way to describe the severity of it all. Seeing is truly believing," Gavin replied. "Let's drive around a bit more. Then we can head back for more research."

"Sounds good. But let's not take too much time before we get back to business."

For the next twenty minutes, Gavin and Marie drove to well-known sites in town. Each time they stopped to look, their surprise continued to grow. It was impossible to see the destruction and simply get used to it or expect it at the next stop. Every major roadway was impassable. Businesses were flooded. Thousands of houses were unlivable. Neither Marie nor Gavin could imagine the personal loss so many were facing at the hands of Mother Nature.

"Turn right up there," Marie said. "I want to see something."

"Okay," Gavin responded but kept driving.

"Hey!" Marie yelled. "I just said to turn. What are you doing? Stop!"

"OK!" Gavin yelled as he slammed on the brakes. "I'm sorry. I thought you meant the next street. Give me more warning next time."

Marie had not been prepared for Gavin to hit the brakes so suddenly. She lurched forward and put her hands against the dashboard to prevent her head from smacking it. "Sheesh!" she yelled. "Are you trying to kill us?"

Before Gavin could respond, Marie realized she was now looking down at the floorboard. Between her feet was a book. "What's this?" she asked as she leaned down to examine it closer.

"What's what?" Gavin asked as he put the car in reverse.

The acceleration of the car caused Marie to lurch yet again. The book at her feet slid a few inches back under the seat. "Stop!" she yelled out. "Stop!"

Gavin was not so quick to stop this time in order to prevent more head-bobbing. Instead, he slowed, put the car in park, and just turned to stare at Marie. "You need to stop yelling at me every time you want me to stop. I'm sorry I missed the turn but I'm doing my best here."

"Shush!" Marie scolded. "Is this a…" she could not finish her sentence.

Marie was quiet. She reached down quickly and grabbed the book at her feet. She turned it over and over in her hands. Then she slowly opened the cover.

September 15, 2013 – 2:30 AM

The ride to Marie's apartment was not quiet. Marie filled the cabin of the car with a cacophony of outbursts, questions, and odd sounds. Gavin held back laughing at her. He knew that would not end well. Once inside her apartment, they tried to bring some calm to the chaos. Gavin sat on the sofa while Marie used a towel to dry her hair.

Marie hollered from the other room, "I know I said this already, but I really think when you picked me up after I crashed my car, this journal fell out of the satchel and slid under the seat. Unfortunately, it has been sitting in your car, still wet from falling out of my car."

"Is any of it legible?"

"Some. The pages are sticking together, and the ink ran in places. As I said on the way here, someone wrote the name Jerry Bekkett inside the cover of the journal. Jerry is Pete's son. It would make sense this is Jerry's journal."

"Will you refresh my memory? When did Jerry live around here?" Gavin asked looking for some historical clarity on the Bekkett family timeline.

"Jerry was born in 1824, back east in Virginia. He moved here with his dad, Pete, his two sisters, and their mom in 1837. Jerry's sons were Luke and Chad. That one journal entry you read yesterday about the mutilated cow was from Luke. Remember?"

"Not gonna forget that one."

Marie continued with the Bekkett timeline, "Pete disappeared in 1860 and Jerry worked on the Bekkett farm with

Luke and Chad until he sold it in 1876. That's when Bekkett became a municipality." After a brief pause, Marie added, "Jerry was...odd."

"How so?"

"Well, he was a recluse. He seemed, um, I guess really mad about his dad's death. It drove him insane. Believe me, I know what it's like to lose a parent. But from historical documents, Jerry was just plain crazy. It was him who seemed to start the stories of some strange beast roaming the region. But just as the stories began with him, they also seemed to end with him. Maybe he came to his senses. Maybe this journal will provide a bit of insight."

"Let's hope," said Gavin. "What happened to Luke and Chad? Maybe they are the ones who brought some sensibility to their dad."

"That's the weird part. I don't think I really know what became of the Bekkett boys," Marie admitted. "I was just relaying much of this same information to Betty when I saw her two days ago. She made a comment about not having all the facts. Do you think...?" Marie trailed off not completing her thoughts.

"Think what?" Before he allowed Marie to answer Gavin made an attempt to finish her thought. "Do you think this one journal will be the magical one answering all of your questions?"

"Well... yes," Marie admitted. "I do wonder if Jerry, strange as he was, would have those missing pieces in his journal. Sometimes it is those reclusive souls that find solace in writing." Marie knew from her own experiences and tribulations that she often wrote down her worst nightmares and thoughts on paper. It was cathartic for her to express her feelings through a pen rather than by speaking them to a stranger.

"It's worth a look. Are the pages dry enough to glean any useful information?" Gavin asked her.

"Whether they are or not, I'm done waiting. I'm going to risk it and start peeling the pages apart."

"Be slow and methodical. No need to rush at this point."

Gavin began scanning the tops of open surfaces in the room. "Hey, have you seen my phone? I don't think I've had it since…" Gavin trailed off. "I guess since yesterday sometime," he finished.

"Um. No. I don't think I've seen it ever. I don't even know what your phone looks like. Is it in your car? Try checking under the seat," she added with a smile.

"Yeah. Thanks. I wouldn't have thought of that!" Gavin responded playfully.

***

Gavin searched the usual places for his phone. The cup holder. The phone holder. The side pocket in his door. "Hello? Phone? Where are you?" Gavin said into the swallowing silence of his car. As he continued his search, he wished the inventor of these great portable devices had created a phone that would respond to the owner asking for its location. *There's probably an app for that* Gavin thought and made a mental note to download it later. As Gavin continued picking through items in his car, he hoped he had not left his phone in the library basement.

***

After Gavin walked outside Marie began the tedious process of separating the wet pages of the journal. It reminded her of coming inside on a snowy day, taking off her boots, and pulling her wet socks off her shins and ankles. She knew if she used too much force with the pages, they would tear apart. She had to be patient and slowly grab the corners of two opposing pages while she carefully pulled one page off the grips of the other.

Marie was able to successfully separate four pages and get a gist of the contents of the journal. Jerry was indeed an unhappy man. "Why are you so mad?" Marie asked the journal hoping she would find a response from the pages within. She continued to peel and read each page. Some pages were not salvageable. But she was able to interpret enough to confirm her historical knowledge was not far out of whack.

Then she reached the mother lode. A block of miraculously dry pages. Her jaw dropped as she raced through a description of events she had never heard before. This was a secret the Bekkett's never divulged. She read the pages while simultaneously picturing a movie in her mind.

August 14, 1873

Double K Ranch

Luke Bekkett knew better than to leave the house as clouds brewed up a storm over the mountains. Within the last two hours, the clouds changed from a wistful light gray into an ominous dark blue. If he were home right now, this worrying change in weather would be followed by orders from his dad, Jerry Bekkett, to go directly inside the house. Today, Luke looked up, held his hands high, and let out a joyful scream in mockery of both the weather and his dad. He spun around until the dust from the ground kicked up with the wind into Luke's nostrils. He coughed, spit onto the ground to clear his throat, then wiped his nose with the sleeve of his shirt.

On Luke's twelfth birthday, Jerry brought Luke outside. He spread his hands wide to indicate the expansive fields of Double K Ranch. It was five thousand acres of mostly fertile soil for crops, rolling hills for exploring, and a creek for cooling off. Jerry stood with his arms spread wide and took in a slow, deep breath. "Now that you're a young man," Jerry told Luke in his gruff voice, "you will need to help me tend the fields. But if it rains, you must get to dry shelter, son." It was a rite of passage Luke's younger brother, Chad, would experience two years later.

The only relief the extra workload of becoming a man brought was finally experiencing the cooling chill that afternoon storms brought to Luke's skin. If rain continued to fall and Luke failed to move to a dry place, he would be shuffled into the protective shelter his paranoid father had built in the middle of their ranch. The wooden structure was no more secure than their outhouse, but somehow Jerry thought the timbers of the small outpost would dissuade the mythical beast from entering. It was, however, no more than a theory as the building's strength had never been tested against the ferocity of any wild animal roaming the plains.

Now, as an independent sixteen-year-old, Luke wandered deep into the fields of the Double K Ranch recalling the tales his parents had spoken of about the beast. The stories rarely changed and there was never proof of their veracity. As Luke grew into a young adult, he believed the stories less and less. But as the sky grew darker, he couldn't shake the idea of a beast that comes alive with the rain. A beast that feeds on the flesh of anything, or anyone, who didn't find dry shelter.

No matter how foolish his parents had seemed during rainstorms, Luke was becoming unnerved at how far he had ventured from the house that afternoon. The clouds blew east, over the caps of the mountains, bringing with them a covering of the sun. Luke silently wished he had told Chad he had left the house. No one knew where he was, and five thousand acres was a lot to cover for a search party of only his brother and dad. He was closer to the shelter than home and headed in that direction.

After ten minutes, what started as mist from the sky were now puddles tumbling on him. He cursed his dad for not building more shelter on the expanse of flat land before him. In his desperation to find shelter, Luke realized his fear of the beast was increasing. After another ten minutes, water permeated Luke's head after soaking through his hat. Tired and wet, Luke sank to his knees. For all the years he doubted the truth of the stories, he laughed at the notion he may become one. Then he swore under his breath for allowing himself to succumb to such foolishness, stood up and walked on. The shelter was not much further, and he could wait out the storm there.

***

"Chad, it's time to get inside. Now!" Jerry repeated the same words every time a few drops of rain fell. Chad was fourteen years old, and, like his older brother, he was tired of his dad's fear of storms. Still, Chad would obey his dad. There was no point for Chad to add to his dad's fears by not going inside. Following Jerry's order, Chad turned toward the house. He paused momentarily as he debated if he should tell his dad he watched Luke wander off nearly three hours earlier. Nothing could be done now, so Chad chose to remain quiet rather than face a litany of angry questions from his dad if he confessed Luke was gone.

***

Luke was startled by a distant screaming. It triggered a distant memory of hearing this same sound once before from the security of his bedroom. At the time it had been so faint he convinced himself it was his imagination. He had been in his bed too frightened to move for fear of waking Chad, who was only seven years old at the time. When Luke finally found the courage to roll to his side, he saw his brother in a catatonic fright and Luke knew Chad had heard it also. They never talked about the startling cries, instead choosing to believe it was the wind howling through the slats of the barn.

But tonight, there was no denying what he heard. It sounded like a hundred third-grade children screaming in unison and lasted longer than humanly possible. The cry was followed by a low, guttural sound. The growl reminded Luke of a mountain lion's warning prior to pouncing on its prey. He stood momentarily paralyzed while trying to determine where the noise originated. He strained his ears and waited for more screams. The rain falling on Luke's hat deafened his senses and he threw the hat aside, not realizing at the time it would be one of the few things of his existence that would ever be found.

***

Chad watched his dad frantically walk the perimeter of the fenced yard. Jerry had set up an area he referred to as the "safe zone." He said it would allow anyone enough time to run into the house before the beast could grip its talons around you. Chad always wondered how a split rail fence would keep a beast of such deathly intent from clawing its way into your flesh. But he did not dare question his father. Chad observed as his dad stepped further away from the safe zone and could not sit quietly any longer.

Chad ran to the front door and opened it. Using his arms as support against the door frame he leaned outside, being sure to keep his feet planted atop the floor inside the house. "Dad! Luke is gone! Please come inside," he pled with his dad.

Jerry ran toward the house. At first, Chad was sure he would be chastised for partially escaping the threshold of the house. Instead, Chad only saw fear take a grip on his father's face. "What do you mean, Luke's gone? Where did he go? When? Why didn't you tell me?" Question after question barraged Chad's face, as his dad's fear matched the strength of the storm.

"I'm sorry, dad. Luke has never gone far before, and I didn't want you to be mad at him. I didn't know it was going to rain."

"It's okay, son. There's nothing we can do now. We must go inside. This rain will awaken the beast. Luke is on his own." His words were dripping with sorrow. Jerry knew Luke would never survive this storm.

***

Luke thought running across a dry, soft dirt field was tiresome work. But navigating through the muddy depths was much worse. With each step, his pace slowed as his feet sank several inches into the water-saturated earth. The thought of being swallowed by the muddy field seemed such a reprieve over running for his life. At this stride, it was only a matter of time before he was captured. He imagined how the beast would gruesomely rip his arms and legs from his torso. He would be forced to helplessly watch and wait until he succumbed to the pain of such torture. It would be a terrifying death unless he could escape.

Luke squinted his eyes to adjust to the dark and he saw the welcoming sight of his dad's shelter fifty yards ahead. It was perched on higher ground than the field and Luke knew maneuvering up the mud-soaked incline would be reminiscent of his day's ice skating at the pond in town. He reached the muddy slope and took two steps up with success. With his third step, he lost his footing and fell face-first into the swampy mess. He pulled his face from the earth, turned his head, and spit dirty water from his mouth. His right ear filled with mud and muffled the scream he heard in the distance. Luke stood and shook the muck from his ears which caused the scream to intensify in volume. It was upon him. Luke turned toward the shelter and hoped for one last chance to escape this nightmare.

As Luke was about to step forward, lightning flashed from on high and silhouetted a figure best described by the apostle John in the book of Revelations. The flash of light seared the image into Luke's memory. The fur of the animal was soaked, yet dense clumps still flopped in the wind. It stood several feet taller than Luke's six-foot, sturdy frame. The length of the extended arms seemed to be equal in length to its legs. Its face, if it had one, was obscured behind hair. He realized the images of the beast his parents spoke of could not have been from first-hand witnesses. In that moment, he understood no true encounters with the beast had left witnesses to speak of this creature's horrific appearance.

Bending over and clawing at the ground, Luke kept his gaze on the horizon. Using his hands, he fumbled on the mucky ground until he found his rifle. He slowly raised the rifle's aim to eye level. He squinted his left eye closed, focused his aim toward the beast, and shot off two rounds. The animal did not flinch or fall over as Luke anticipated. Instead of screams of agony, the beast seemed to smile as its hair was ripped from its body by the bullets. Luke stared straight ahead, readying his aim for another shot. His finger was on the trigger waiting for the next flash of light to provide him the illumination he needed for a head shot. When the moment came and the sky lit with brilliance, the beast was gone. Luke sighed in relief and fell to the ground gasping for breath. His nightmare was over.

***

Jerry and Chad set out at daybreak, hoping they would not need the entire day to find Luke, yet preparing for the maximum amount of light and good weather. The rain had stopped in the middle of the night with the ground soaking up the moisture like a thirsty sponge, then spitting the excess water back to the surface creating puddles and sinkholes that littered the landscape. Saddling their horses, they knew the trek would be slow as they would need to navigate carefully to avoid muddy sinkholes. Knowing Luke's best chance at survival was the shelter, Jerry and Chad silently pointed the horses in that direction.

Navigating through rows of still growing crops, they came upon Luke's hat. It sat as an island in the sea of muddy water. The brim of the hat ominously pointed west, toward the shelter, and the men continued their search. The field which hosted the shelter was long and narrow and the crops planted within were no more than two feet high. It provided a clear view from one end to the other. As Jerry and Chad rounded the bend of the river, they could immediately see shreds of wood scattered on the ground. The men prodded the horses to a faster trot, careful to keep their feet from sinking into the field. Within a few feet of the shelter, Jerry moved his gaze from the horizon to something in the field that caught his attention. He focused his eyes and pulled on the reins of the horse to pull it to a sudden stop. Jerry jumped from his horse with his feet making a thudding noise as his boots were sucked into the grips of the mud. At the same time, Chad cried out an unintelligible sound.

Both men saw Luke's rifle lying in pieces on the plod of ground at the base of the steps leading up to the now twisted pile of wood. A breeze pushed the wisps of hair off Chad's forehead and simultaneously blew the cloud cover away. The clarity of the sunshine revealed the worst. The water the men were wading through was red. The clumps of grass were hair. Luke was gone. Jerry fell prostrate on the ground wailing. Every warning he had given Luke had been in vain. He sat up, turned toward Chad, and screamed in agony. Chad did not need to know specific words. The emotions his dad displayed clearly spoke volumes. He turned his horse and galloped off unable to see through the tears in his eyes.

September 15, 2013 – 2:40 AM

     Marie sat in stunned silence in disbelief at what she had just pieced together. A tear began to form in the corner of her left eye as she replayed the vision of Luke's horrific death. She could not put the journal down now and continued to peel apart more pages. When she turned to the next partially legible page of Jerry's journal, she read on.

I loathe my dad for bringing us here. His greed killed him, and my beloved Luke. Curse you, Pete Bekkett! You always blamed Weston, but the real blame, the real person who wanted wealth and fame more than Weston was you. You deserved your fate. Luke did not. The Bekkett's do not deserve this wrath we face. A secret we must hide. I'm tired of hiding the truth for you. I'm tired of mourning the loss of Luke and the thoughts of how he died.

     "Oh my gosh!" she exclaimed. "No wonder you were bitter. Your dad disappeared and now your son is dead in some terrible manner. What else are you hiding, Jerry?" Marie asked no one in particular.

     She continued to separate pages, which mostly displayed blurred words. Marie silently cursed under her breath knowing so much truth had been blotted away from this journal due to her carelessness. Several pages later Marie was able to read more of Jerry's writings.

It's done. Chad and I finally found success in burying... She could not piece together the letters, and then read on. *Our years of labor...* Again, the words were illegible. Marie scanned to the next set of words she could decipher. *No one will ever suffer again.*

Before she had time to process the totality of what she discovered, Gavin burst into the apartment. Marie jumped again at his loud entrance. *When will he learn to calm down when approaching me while I'm doing research?* Marie was about to verbalize her internal dialogue when she looked up and saw a look of horror on Gavin's face.

"What's wrong, Gavin? Is your dad okay?" Marie asked desperate for an answer.

Gavin was in a daze. He had his phone in his hand and was staring at its screen. He was not speaking, and Marie knew something was wrong. "Gavin?" she asked trying to shake him from his daze. "Gavin?"

"Hmm?" was all Gavin could say.

"You're scaring me. What happened?" Marie prodded.

Gavin turned his phone toward Marie. He had no words to accompany the action.

Marie understood his gesture and looked at the screen. "Holy..." Marie continued her statement with a four-letter word. "What the hell is that? Is it? Where did you get that? I can't believe it. It's... it's real!" Marie finally said.

"It is real. And I think it ate Taylor," Gavin said coldly. "He sent this to me yesterday. I remember seeing he sent a text. I just never opened it until now. The file was too large to upload without an internet connection," Gavin added with a matter-of-fact tone.

"I'm sorry, Gavin," Marie said with genuine remorse. "I know you and Taylor were close. But why...?" she couldn't finish her question. She knew why Gavin thought he was dead. There was no possible way to get a picture that close and live to speak about it.

"This whole time!" Gavin began yelling. "This whole time we have been in the basement searching for clues. And… and the answer was on my phone. This whole time!" Gavin kept repeating. "If only I had answered his text."

"And then what?" Marie asked. "You would magically head on over to Taylor's place and save him? He was dead moments after he sent that. Gavin, there's nothing you could have done differently that would have saved Taylor."

"But what if…" Gavin trailed off again. He was having a difficult time coming up with complete sentences. "What if I had known sooner?"

Marie moved toward Gavin and gave him a hug knowing little she could say would bring comfort like a reassuring embrace. Marie then stepped back and looked into his glossy eyes.

"You didn't know sooner, and you can't change the timing of this or the outcome. What has happened has happened. Trust me. I know what it is like to wish for a different outcome. I know what it is like to wonder if you could have made a difference and changed one event in hopes of saving those you love. Gavin, nothing you did, or did not do, would have had an impact."

"I just…" Gavin again did not finish his thought.

"When did he send that? And where was he?" Marie asked Gavin hoping to get him to open up and start thinking again.

"Um. I dunno. Let me check." Gavin looked at his phone and continued, "Looks like I received this at four eighteen yesterday afternoon. Oh, man!" Gavin continued. "I saw this text when I went to Lefty's, but it wouldn't load, and I didn't want to wait. I was too busy with other things. What if…"

"What if nothing!" Marie interrupted. "Gavin nothing would have stopped this. Maybe we would have had an answer to this mystery a lot earlier. But you did not make this happen. It is not your fault."

Gavin looked at his phone again. "There's a message from my dad. Do you think he knows about Taylor? Maybe he knows more," Gavin added.

"Let me see," said Marie as she gently took the phone from Gavin's grasp. "Sit down for a minute and I'll check your phone." As she read over the messages, her mouth involuntarily opened.

"What?" asked Gavin. "What did my dad say?"

"Just a minute," Marie answered as she continued to peruse several messages. "It seems your dad has some weird hunch about something bad happening in town. He didn't clarify what, exactly, but did say he mapped out several missing persons and animals. It looks like people along the path of the flood reported loud screams and missing pets. A few missing people too."

"Are you serious?!" Gavin squawked.

"Yes," Marie said flatly. "I am very serious. It appears your dad is finally questioning all the decades-old stories and wondering if there is more here than meets the eye."

"My dad. Who woulda thought?"

"There's nothing more his words will tell us now. We know the truth," Marie said.

"Like hell there's nothing my dad's word won't add to this!" Gavin interjected. "He knows where this... where the beast is roaming. He knows its path. I don't know how that helps, exactly, but it does tell us something we would never have known on our own."

"You're right," Marie admitted. "I'm sorry. It is great information. I guess the better question is what do we do with this knowledge?"

"Steve," Gavin said simply.

"Who is Steve?"

"Pastor Steve. You know him?"

"From Rising Son?"

"Yes. He's not just a pastor. He's a friend," Gavin told her. "We need to get to the church and talk to Steve. Maybe he can help us. I don't know, but I feel like this thing is so much bigger than you or I can handle on our own."

"I guess," Marie said not really wanting to include anyone else on this journey. She knew now was not a good time to tell Gavin to set his feelings aside. If he needed to speak to Steve, she knew she would have to be patient. "Let me grab this journal and we can go now. I'll read more on our way to the church."

"Well, actually, I was hoping you would drive. I need to call my dad."

With a silent sigh, Marie took the keys to Gavin's car from his hand. She held onto the journal just in case she had some spare time at the church to continue reading the pages within.

***

Marie adjusted the seat and mirrors to match her smaller frame. Once settled in, she turned her head and looked at Gavin. "Buckle up, buddy."

"Why? Are you planning on driving my car into a ditch too?"

"Not cool. Not cool at all." Marie lightly punched Gavin on his left arm.

"Yeah. I deserved that. Okay, I'm gonna call my dad now."

"Will you put it on speakerphone? I want to hear what he says."

Even though his dad's number was on speed dial, Gavin chose to take a few more seconds and manually push in the digits. He feared there would be a lot to process and he was subconsciously delaying the conversation. The phone did not even ring on Gavin's side of the call when he heard his dad answer with a hello that oozed with obvious relief that Gavin was finally returning his calls and texts.

"Hey, dad. Just now got all your messages. Like I told you earlier, Marie and I were in the basement and had no cell service down there."

"I know. I'm just glad you called me back. Can you meet me at the EOC?"

"No. We're on our way to Rising Son to meet with Steve. You'll have to tell me what you found out. Maybe send me a pic or two."

"I really wish we could talk in person, but I guess this will have to do. Give me a minute. I need to find somewhere a bit more private." Gavin could hear muffled noises and guessed his dad had covered the phone with his hand rather than pushing the mute button. Then, "You still there, Gavin?"

"Yep. Still here. Listen, dad. I'm actually very excited to hear what you've discovered. But I'm gonna need the very abbreviated version. I've only got about ten minutes."

"This is a bit bigger than a short conversation, son."

"Do your best."

"I overheard our call-takers receiving a bunch of calls about missing people and pets. Along with the missing was an odd yelling or screaming noise from outside somewhere. I took the info from the calls, grabbed a map, and pinpointed where each report occurred. For the most part, it was all along the river. Before you say anything, Gavin, I know how silly it all sounds. I get it that things will go missing along a flood path. But this just feels different."

"Okay. What else do you have?" Gavin continued his flat, dull tone with his dad which betrayed the internal thoughts spinning in his head.

"I know you and Marie are hot on the trail of some news story. I know you were out at Double K Ranch. I know the stories of the Bekkett Beast and the screaming that people supposedly heard. Beyond that, I don't really know what it all means."

"Sir, this is Marie," she spoke up a bit louder than necessary hoping Tom could hear her. "You're on speakerphone. We know the beast is real. We haven't pieced it all together yet, but…" Marie trailed off for a minute. "But we have proof."

"You have proof?!" Tom nearly yelled. "How? Is it out there right now?"

Before answering Tom's question, Gavin asked one of his own. "Dad. Did you get any reports from Stagecoach Lane? Or somewhere in that general area?"

Tom paused as he scanned the map in front of him. "Some guy called in from 49102 Stagecoach Lane. Hang on, let me scan the notes." There was a pause while Tom looked over the report in front of him. "Seems he saw a body floating in the water. The call taker states he was rude and hung up when he was told the police could not get out there. Why?"

"That's where our proof originated. Taylor took a picture of something. And it's not something from this earth."

"How did he get a picture? What did he say about it?"

"He's dead, dad. He has to be. There is no way he got as close as he did and lived."

"Taylor is a resourceful guy, Gavin. I'm sure he is still alive."

Marie joined the conversation again and said, "With all due respect, Tom, given everything we have ever been told about this thing, all the stories, and what we have learned today, well, there's no way Taylor is still alive."

Silence consumed both sides of the phone for several seconds.

"Dad. We are almost to the church. I need to know where you last tracked this thing."

"Why? I can't have you go hunting it down and getting killed. No way."

"You called to tell me about this for a reason. We have to know where it's headed. I don't have a plan and I certainly am not interested in being its next meal. Please, tell us what you know."

After a few seconds of silence, Marie added, "Tom, please help us out."

With a heavy sigh, Tom finally said, "I cannot believe I'm doing this. The path is from west to east, mostly along Sand Creek's former path. That's a lot wider path now with all the flooding. The last report came from someone who heard what they said was a loud raucous coming from the Sugar Mill. The same person called a few minutes after their first call and said it had quieted and sounded like it moved east."

"It's almost out of Bekkett's town limits, then," Gavin said.

"Gavin. Marie. Be safe. Keep me posted. Do not do anything stupid. I love you, Gavin."

"We are at the church. Gotta go. We will be very safe." With no more thought about reciprocating his dad's love, Gavin pushed the red button on his phone. Before Marie could add any comments to the abruptly ended conversation, Gavin unbuckled his seatbelt and stepped out of the car.

September 15, 2013 – 4:00 AM

It was not unusual for a church building to be full of people on a Sunday morning. But at this early hour, the crowds were mostly sleeping on cots in the gymnasium turned hostel. Marie and Gavin wandered up and down several hallways searching for Steve. Out of respect for those slumbering, they remained quiet and decided not to ask around. It only then occurred to Gavin he should have called first. For all he knew Steve was at home sleeping and preparing for the day ahead. Marie stopped after five minutes of futile searching.

"So far we have established Steve is not in the gym, the lobby, nor any of these three hallways. He's probably in his office. Guide us there. That's our best option, Gavin."

"Good thinking. I'm a bit frazzled. It's this way," he said with a wave of his hand.

The only light in the offices was from the entryway lamp set on its lowest setting. Just enough light to guide footsteps away from obstacles. Dark enough to provide a private sanctuary if anyone were trying to sleep here. Gavin hoped that was what Steve was doing now. He did not want to waste any more time trying to find his friend. He was questioning why he came here in the first place and may choose to carry on their search without Steve if he was not found soon.

Gavin pushed open Steve's door while simultaneously tapping on it with his knuckle. He realized in that moment it may be a poor idea to enter and scare Steve into doing some kung-foo move on Gavin in his startled state of mind. Gavin decided to also whisper, "Hey, Steve. Steve? You awake? It's Gavin. And Marie."

Steve sat up from his reclined position on the sofa and rubbed his face with his hand wiping away the sleep. He then ran his hand through his moppy head of hair and said, "Come on in," with a tone that indicated he had been waiting all along for this meeting. In reality, Steve was still a bit groggy and trying to comprehend why his friend was standing in his doorway at such an early hour.

***

Marie told the Bekkett history for a third time in as many days. Only this time she added a few more pieces of information even though she wondered if Steve would think her crazy. She relayed what little information she had about Weston and Lady Okayo, and how she may have unimaginably brought rain and maybe a beast to the area. Because Steve knew the Bible, she also told him about the Asherah Pole and how this seemed eerily similar.

As Marie spoke passionately about her theories and ideas, Steve stood from his recliner and paced near his office window. Occasionally, he paused, placed his palms on his desk, and looked at the floor. A few sighs or hushed tones escaped his lips every now and then. Marie was unsure if Steve was listening intently or waiting for her to conclude so he could tell her how crazy she was.

The moment Marie wrapped up her story, Steve said bluntly, "I know what is happening." His words were flat and emotionless and almost did not register in Marie's mind.

"Yes, it's raining. And it's of Biblical proportions. It is on a scale like only Egypt and Moses could fully understand," Marie quipped with sarcasm and a slight bit of rage. She was guessing Steve was about to start preaching and she just did not want to hear it today. "And the weather has created temporary insanity within me."

"Not the rain, Marie. And you're certainly not insane. I know what happens when it rains. The people who suffer."

"Wait. What?" Marie was stammering. Her brain was too jumbled with information from the past few days to fully understand what Steve meant.

Gavin held up his hand toward Marie to indicate he would deal with his so-called friend's rude reaction. "Steve," Gavin interrupted. "This is not the time nor place to conjecture. Leave Marie alone. We have been through a lot. You need to really hear the words she just spoke. Let it soak in for a second."

"Oh. It's soaking in. I wasn't standing here wondering how crazy Marie is. I was in shock." Steve paused to gather his thoughts. Slowly he continued, "I fully believe this is not speculation, you two. It is quite possibly the scariest reality any of us have ever faced."

"What?" Gavin whispered. He knew when he walked into Steve's office this was a gamble and a risk to tell anyone else their crazy notion of a beast stalking the community.

Steve looked back and forth between his guests, meeting each eye-to-eye. "I'm afraid it is the cold hard facts, Marie." He waited for a response, but both stared right back at Steve. He clarified, "Straight from Betty Bekkett."

"When? How? What?" Marie flung her questions at Steve. She was an empty cup waiting to be filled with knowledge of this thing. This beast. The artifact she had chased and hunted for so long.

Marie stood and approached Steve. Then she stopped, turned around, and sat down. She put her head into her hands and let out a deep breath. She finally looked up and said, "I don't understand."

"Betty came to see me at the church two days ago," Steve began.

Marie quickly cut in. "When? *I* was with Betty two days ago! She didn't say anything about meeting with you. In fact, she and I had plans and she canceled on me. Wait, are you the reason she canceled? You stole the one great chance I had at discovering the truth!"

"Are you finished?" Steve replied.

"I'm sorry."

Gavin spoke up to defend Marie's exasperation. "Marie has been overwhelmed as of late. This mystery has not just been her life-long mission to uncover. The past two days she has wrecked her car, plastered papers over her apartment walls, sat in a basement for hours, and missed a historic rainstorm in search of the answers."

"Search no more," Steve said. "I think I know everything. Will you two stop talking long enough to allow me to tell you what Betty confessed?

"I'm sorry," Marie and Gavin said in unison.

Steve sat back in his chair and mused how he was about to confess in his own office – something others generally did while he listened. "I'm guessing by now, after all you've told me of this storm, Betty isn't with us. She's in a much better place. Somewhere she will no longer need to keep the truth locked away.

"Betty came to my office to declare the truth. To tell me something so outrageous and odd it wasn't until this moment I even believed it was genuine. I picked up the phone to call Adult Protective Services several times. I was hoping they could take her to be evaluated for her mental health. It turns out, she wasn't lying. She wasn't embellishing the truth. She was unburdening herself from a weight no one should carry."

Steve paused for a minute gathering his thoughts. "Marie, you mentioned a man named Weston, is that right?"

"Yes," Marie said tentatively.

"I know who he is. And I do not like him. This carnage..." Steve trailed off for a moment thinking of how many lives would forever be changed after this storm. "This carnage is a result of Weston's greed. He was the real owner of this land." Steve spread his arms as wide as he could to indicate the land incorporating Bekkett and the surrounding area. "Weston's wealth came because of his ability to farm and work with the indigenous people of the area. But a severe drought hit the region, and he suffered immensely. His cattle died. His crops withered. His workers fled. His family was falling apart."

Gavin put up his hand to ask a question. Steve nodded his head and Gavin asked, "Did Betty tell you all of this?"

"Yes. This is from Betty herself."

Steve waited for more questions. After hearing none, he continued.

"This is where it gets a bit crazy. It was at this part when Betty was telling me about her family's history, that I contemplated calling the authorities to have her mental stability checked out. She said while Weston was losing everything around him, he was, quite obviously, concerned about his ability to survive the drought. But one thing he had was his servant. This servant was a witch doctor, so to speak. From what Betty told me, that lady sounds like the devil reincarnate if you ask me."

Marie now raised her hand. Steve looked at both of them and chuckled. "This isn't class. You don't need to raise your hands. But, go ahead, Marie."

"Would that be Lady Okayo? The one we heard mentioned in the journals."

"Yes, it was. As the earth continued to get scorched, Weston begged her to use her Haitian magic. His lust for power was strong, as was hers, and he demanded she create a solution to the lack of water. He told her he was done waiting for God, or whomever, to send rain and asked her to bring the clouds and rain back to his lands.

"She used the dust of the earth to fulfill Weston's request. She conjured something so horrific, that even he wasn't prepared for what was created. Like the Old Testament idols, like the Asherah poles so frequently worshipped in hopes of fertile soil, Lady Okaya spit in the dusty earth, stirred it with her stick, said a prayer, and a beast was born. That is what is haunting us today, my friends."

Marie couldn't move. She could not speak. She could barely think. She allowed Steve's words to fill every gap in her mind that had been void of the truth. As his words sunk in, she was flooded with thoughts. Too many to articulate.

"If Weston and Lady Okayo died, how do we know any of that is true?"

"Weston's right-hand man witnessed the entire thing. He rode off to the Bekkett's the night this happened and told them. Betty said the Bekkett's murdered him and took control of Weston's possessions."

"So, it's true," was all Marie could muster.

"I am afraid it is," Steve replied. "The stories we have all been told when we were kids were merely rewritten versions of the truth to protect those who really knew."

Gavin finally spoke up. "It makes no sense. The Bekkett's could not keep such a story secret for so long. And why didn't they get eaten or die? There's no way this is true. Betty was old and senile. She told you a story in the hopes of keeping her name afloat when she knew a flood would sink her property." Even as he spoke the words, he was not fully convinced he believed them himself.

The spinning of Marie's head was beginning to slow. "No, Gavin. It does make sense!" Marie was animated and stood up to continue her thought. "It makes perfect sense. We found the deed of paper. It was for the land. Your theory was almost spot on. The Bekkett's didn't kill Weston but knew he had been killed. They used that knowledge to silently steal the land from Weston's family. Obviously, he had no need for it anymore. And then, they used this beast to plant new crops, buy new livestock, and build their fortune. They thrived on his misfortune. I think they are almost worse than Weston!"

Gavin piped up, "But I don't understand where the beast went for all these years. If they somehow managed to kill it, how is it alive today?"

Steve chimed in again. "That's the problem. And it is the *real* reason Betty was here the other day. She needed to tell someone. I think she had a premonition or some sort of knowledge this storm was going to be far worse than any of us expected. She told me more."

"We're listening," said Gavin. Marie sat in the chair again.

"The Bekkett's knew they could not continue keeping such a great secret. They also seemed to gain some moral integrity and knew the killing had to cease. They planned for several years how to kill the beast but failed miserably on multiple occasions. Not knowing exactly how they would kill the beast, they decided to create a tomb, of sorts, for it to live within. They spent several more years digging a hole in their field and encasing it with bricks and mortar.

"Wondering how they would ever capture the creature, God seemed to step in to aid with their dilemma. Another drought occurred. The beast did not survive. They found its lifeless body in their field and dragged it to the catacombs they had built. After placing the beast inside, they covered it with dirt and more bricks and mortar. They were convinced the evil would cease to terrorize the land."

"I just read bits and pieces of that in Jerry's journal. It makes so much more sense now! Burying the beast did work for decades!" Marie exclaimed. "It stayed hidden... Is that what Betty was going to show me? The beast's tomb?"

"I doubt she was going to open it up and invite you inside for a special viewing," Gavin said. "But maybe she was going to share the news with you."

"How did it get out?" Marie wondered.

There was silence in the office as the three of them pondered this question. Gavin spoke up and said, "My dad told me the storm was so violent and so sudden, the river created new passageways in the land. The riverbanks no longer chose the path for the water. The water chose its own destiny. It opened up new lands to become rivers and lakes. I bet it ripped right through the catacomb of the beast. I mean, the river wraps around the Double K Ranch and it could easily have split the field in half."

Continuing with what little logic could be made from this situation, Marie added, "And the lady from the National Guard also said the water created its own pathways. We saw for ourselves the torrent that covered the golf course and buried that neighborhood. I'd say anything's possible at this point."

Steve chimed in again. "I'm going to have to agree with your theory. We have to assume the water ripped into the tomb and covered the beast with the very thing it needs to thrive. Water. Once revived, the beast went on a rampage to make up for lost time."

"So many missing people and pets," Gavin said solemnly. "Do you think the beast ate them all?"

"Probably not," Steve said. "Some of them are missing at the hands, or jowls, of the beast. But I'm sure others were washed away or may have simply left before this even happened."

"Now that we know this, what do we do?" Marie asked the men. "We have a responsibility to stop this thing. We cannot sit back and do nothing."

Steve and Gavin had no immediate answers. Then Steve spoke up. "We have to confront it. Gavin, you said your dad told you its last known location, right?"

"Yes."

"Great!" Steve turned on his computer and pulled up a map of the region. "From what he said, plot out where the reports came from, starting from the earliest report to the most recent."

"I didn't get a detailed report. He said it was following the path of Sand Creek and the last report was east of the Sugar Mill." Gavin took hold of the mouse and clicked on various points along the river from Double K Ranch to the Sugar Mill. As he concluded, he stepped back and the three of them scanned the plot points looking for further clues that may indicate the beast's intended path.

Marie spoke first, "We know it is following the old Sand Creek, for the most part. Starting on the west side of town. Heading east."

"When was the last sighting, Gavin?" Steve asked.

"I don't know exactly when, but I would guess sometime within the last hour.

"That's where we need to go then," said Steve.

"Where?" Marie asked.

"There," this time Steve pointed to the map on his screen. "Garden Park. It's the easternmost portion of town. The park sits above the water level and should still be intact."

September 15, 2013 – 5:15 AM

Gavin, Marie, and Steve left the sanctity of the church and piled into Gavin's car. They hadn't formulated a plan but agreed they would develop one during the ride to Garden Park. As soon as he put his car in drive, Gavin asked, "Who could do this? I mean, who thought creating such a hideous creature was a good way to bring rain?"

Steve answered, "This was created by someone who was desperate. Someone hollow inside. Someone who reflected on their life and realized they had nowhere to turn. That person saw a future he had hoped to accomplish and realized it was never going to happen at that moment in time. Weston was empty, sad, and lonely. I would argue that he was broken and unable to clearly see the good he had. He focused only on the negative.

"You can blame his mistakes or recognize you, too, may have felt the same as Weston. In the moment of despair, it is easy to look around and see what you don't have. Then you look within and hope to fill that void. His lust for something greater masked the reality of what was in front of him. He was facing a temporary challenge and sought an immediate solution."

Gavin reflected on Steve's words. "Okay. You're saying Weston feared losing everything he had worked for. And in that moment of fear, he chose an alternative that he thought would return his fortune? So, why didn't they just conjure up a storm?"

"A rainstorm would have had no consequences for his greed. If you're going to gain something, you must sacrifice for it to have meaning. Lady Okayo knew that. She wasn't going to simply give Weston water."

There was a pause in conversation as the three looked out the car windows at the empty streets. Steve took in a deep breath momentarily filling the silence. "Marie's a sharp woman. She made a great connection earlier to this beast and the Asherah idol from the Old Testament. Asherah was a fertility goddess. The Bekkett Beast is a fertility idol. Nothing more."

"Idols don't kill!" Gavin said sharply. He was beginning to doubt the sanity of driving toward the beast.

"What is an idol?" Steve asked, waiting for an answer. "You can answer that one, Gavin. Or Marie." Steve turned his head over his shoulder. Marie had been sitting silently in the backseat.

"I guess an idol is anything you hold as value over something else?" Her tone was more of a question than an answer. For years she had sought the truth of this beast. Her search for answers had become her idol. Until this moment, she never realized the implications of that connection.

"Not bad, but not quite what I was thinking. An idol is something you covet. It's a desire to be like someone or something. So much so that you're willing to take power away from yourself and lay it in the hands of your idol. And in giving the power to another, you end up feeling wounded and broken. In essence, you concede your capability to live in freedom."

"Again," Gavin said, "Idols don't kill, and this thing is mutilating every living thing in its path!"

"Think about it, Gavin. What gives any idol its power?" Steve asked.

"Are we seriously going to have a Q and A session?!"

"Humor me, Gavin."

"This is ridiculous," Gavin harrumphed. There was a lull in conversation and Gavin felt pressure to fill the air. "I guess, based on what you're saying, an idol would feed off the pleasure others give it. And in feeding its pleasure, which in this case is *killing people*, it gains power. And the fear it brings with each death takes away our freedom to live in peace. Am I on the right track here, Steve?"

"Absolutely! People one hundred years ago gave this beast its power. The people fed this beast. And when the masses feed their idol's desire, the idol increases in power. Is this starting to make sense?" Steve asked Marie and Gavin.

"Sort of," Marie answered. "I'm just taking this all in. It changes how I've thought about the beast."

Conversation waned as they each processed their thoughts of what they were about to face. The tires rolling over the wet pavement caused a sloshing noise on the floorboard of the car. The white noise of the roadway kept them all quiet as Gavin navigated toward the park. After a few moments Steve quietly said, "A century ago, Weston and the Bekkett's were willing to set aside reason and sanity to fulfill their own lust for water. Water they needed to fuel their livelihood. The same water the beast needed to fuel its craving for blood.

"The three of us are no different than the previous generation. We push aside the ugly characteristics we don't want others to see. We feverishly try to forget the memories and feelings that remind us we carry pain and shame. Sometimes it is pain we caused and want to forget. Sometimes it's pain that brutally beat us down as we desperately tried to fight it off. But ultimately, it is pain that we have never rid ourselves of. Pain that has been steering us throughout our lives. Pain that has been given power. Power that has taken away our freedom. When you're ready to expose that pain – only then will it lose its effectiveness at being a cancerous cyst that has been growing inside you."

At this, Marie piped up. "So, when the Beckett's buried the creature, they were doing nothing more than pushing it aside in hopes to forget about its existence. But they never truly destroyed it. And now it's back."

Gavin turned the car into the small parking lot purposefully slowing to a crawl to delay their arrival. It was dark and the rain had let up. There were no other vehicles in the lot and Gavin said, "Looks like we're the only foolish ones here."

Unfortunately, with this degree of isolation, it would limit the beast's menu choices to three. *These are not good odds* Marie thought as she looked around the area for any signs of the beast.

"Steve, what's the plan? You're the military guy. This seems more in your wheelhouse than ours," Gavin said. "How are three unarmed and untrained people going to contain a beast that has caused mass casualties during this storm?" Gavin asked.

"Two untrained. I trained with the best men and women in the world. But, none of that matters. We could have every Navy Seals team here with us now and that show of force would not be enough to kill this beast," Steve said.

"Then how, exactly, are *we* going to destroy this thing? And destroy it so it never returns?" Gavin asked. "We didn't bring this sick thing to life. How do the three of us have the power to destroy it? Don't we need a Bekkett here to end the cycle of violence they were a part of?"

"That's a logical question," Steve admitted. "But that's not how this works. As a counselor, I see a lot of people who struggle with a lot of pain. Many of those people were abused at the hands of others. They didn't create the pain, but they have the power to put an end to it."

Gavin was worked up. "But still, the pain began in their presence and can end in their presence. Regardless of their role in its creation, they were there. None of us were roaming these desolate plains when some idiot thought it a great idea to bring it here. So, what authority do we have to rid our town of the beast right now?"

"Steve, may I attempt an answer?" Marie looked directly at Steve for permission to bring sense to Gavin's stubbornness.

Steve lifted his hands, palms up, handing the conversation to Marie. "Please."

"Gavin, I already told you about my trip to Israel. Ya know, the Israelites wandering the desert and the Asherah Pole example?"

"Yes..." Gavin said while simultaneously prodding her for more information.

"They demanded a king lead them. They wanted to be like the tribes and countries surrounding them. They were looking for physical leadership, not just an unseen God to follow."

Marie paused waiting for some sort of acknowledging tone from Gavin. When he did not provide any reassurance, Marie prodded him. "Are you with me, Gavin?"

"Carry on," he said.

"Micah was a prophet from the Old Testament. I know, I know. You've already told me you read the New Testament more than the Old, so you may not be familiar with him."

"Well, I've still heard of Micah," Gavin interjected even though he was straining the annals of his mind to remember the name.

"The relevance from the Old Testament is very tangible today. Even though the kings had been appointed with good intentions, many of them fell from grace and turned toward idol worship. It was much easier for the people to pray to a life-size, tangible object than to follow whispers in their heads. They wanted to see power, not merely feel it. That's what Steve is telling us. It is so much easier to turn our attention toward physical admiration rather than focus on the unseen."

"I can't argue with you on that," Gavin agreed.

"Good but let me finish. Micah did not create nor condone the idol worship the kings were allowing. He emphatically warned against poor decisions that would open the door to evil intentions. Micah profoundly stated the ignorant leaders had become very good at accomplishing very bad things in their society. Micah warned against the rise of the powerful and the destruction they were causing. He could have fled. He could have stayed quiet. He knew he was safe and would not fall victim to the chaos of the kings. Instead, he chose to stand strong and voice his concerns. He made a conscious decision to intercede on behalf of all those who were suffering the consequences of the choices only a few had made." Marie paused, looked at the ground for a moment, then met Gavin's eyes. "I don't know exactly what that means. I just see a correlation here."

As Marie wrapped up her words, she pulled on the door handle, opened it, and stood up. The air was cool and a slight breeze hugged her arms. She reached back into the car and pulled on her sweater, but the chill of the night was already seizing her bones. There was no escaping or shrouding her fear.

Both men exited the car and stood. Steve spread his feet apart and bent down. He reached his hands toward his back and let out a satisfying sigh as he stretched his muscles. "I didn't realize how tense I was until I stood up."

Before Gavin or Marie could answer, a distant scream filled the night air. The three hushed their voices and simultaneously turned their heads toward the west.

September 15, 2013 – 5:45 AM

The creature heard their arrival at the park. It sent out a quick burst of a scream to announce its presence. It was a short yell, yet long enough to fill its prey with fear at its pending arrival. The beast knew from past meals their fear would paralyze them from fighting back. It would be guaranteed a savory meal. Crouching, it moved slowly through the moist field inching closer to the three. The weeds were slapping lightly at the shins of each leg dampening its fur, bringing with it the life-giving water it needed. As its furry mass moved closer, it slowly climbed a tree, ever so quiet. It would hunt its prey tonight with deliberate purpose. Killing each one first, then returning to their limp bodies to devour and savor the flesh.

To many, the beast was nothing more than a hideous sight bringing death. But it had thoughts and it could sense pain and fear in those it sought. The beast also knew a lack of fear in its prey could be used against it, which is why it always struck first. The beast also had memories and remembered the night it was created. On a dry, hot night, Lady Okayo performed her magic well. She created evil to alleviate the fears of a drought. Their worry of cropless fields fled as the rain fell. Their terror of death by mutilation grew with each new death discovered. It fed, lived, and thrived off those fears.

It also remembered its capture and entombment. It lay buried for a century awaiting its resurrection. This storm's power enlivened the beast with an unsatiable appetite. It vowed to never face defeat again. The beast reached its perch atop the tree and tilted its head toward the conversation.

***

The scream had been short lived with no other noises. They turned back toward one another. "It is time for us to recognize our own internal struggles and to lay them down in front of us. This beast feeds on exposing flesh and bones. And it will die when we expose our internal beasts. Laying down our pain and suffering will cause the creature out there to suffer, whither, and decay." Steve was now pointing toward the scream they had heard moments earlier.

It was Marie's turn to add a comment. "So, what you are saying, Steve, if I'm following you here, is we have to empty the brokenness of ourselves to drain the beast's power?"

"That's right," Steve responded. "But we don't rid ourselves of pain, bad memories, hurtful stares, financial loss, or words spoken against us by merely burying it deep inside. Humans are great at burying the truth. But those feelings remain. Hidden, under the surface. It is exactly those wounds we hope to forget when we give power to our idols. When all we do is bury experiences and move on, we are always painfully aware of their existence."

As Steve's message began to register with both Marie and Gavin, the night grew eerily quiet. The rain had been falling for so long now, that the absence of water pattering the ground became very noticeable. There was a stillness in the air implying even the wind had fled in fear of the beast's destructive power. All three needed to fully understand what he was saying if they had any chance to defeat their enemy. Steve allowed the silence to encase them.

Gavin now jumped into the conversation. "If I'm hearing Steve correctly, he's saying we must face the beast like we *should* face our own internal struggles and expose it for what it is – an idol. Or some sort of means to an end that was created out of fear and pain and desperation."

"Yes!" Steve yelled. Realizing the folly of speaking so loudly, he hushed his voice, "If we merely bury this beast again, if we could even be so lucky as to manage that, it will rise eventually. It will bring terror and destruction to future generations. The destruction must be permanent.

"But I believe the only way to fight terror of supernatural means is by opening our own wounds and exposing those things we have held onto that have kept us as ineffective members of society. Examine your brokenness. Examine those things which you turn to when you want to hide from your shame. There is something inside that you must recognize and unleash in order to defeat the evil that is before us."

"Okay, Steve. You are freaking me out, here. We have no weapons. Yes, you are a one-legged stud, but do you want us to simply "think" this thing into non-existence? It makes no sense!"

Steve needed to calm Gavin's thoughts. He slowed the pace of his words and lowered his voice to a near whisper. He knew if his words were soft, Gavin would match the tone. "The beast was conjured out of fear. It will be conquered despite our fear. By the power only God can release."

Gavin subconsciously matched Steve's tone and hushed volume and calmly continued the dialogue. "I'm still confused, Steve. Am I supposed to sit quietly in meditation and simply pray for God to kill this thing? I can pretty much guarantee the people terrorized in the 1800s were saying their share of prayers. How will mine today be any different?"

Marie jumped into the conversation. "Because we're not merely praying. Steve's not telling us to throw out some holy words or Hail Mary. This is self-examination. We're not going to allow the beast to tear us apart. We have to do that to ourselves. Symbolically speaking, of course."

"Of course," Steve agreed.

"Gavin, you wondered what authority you have right here and now. Just like Micah had no direct authority to stop the destruction caused by the leaders of his time, you also have no authority. Only God carries that. Have you ever been at church when they made an altar call?" Steve asked.

"Yes, but I never budged out of my seat," Gavin confessed.

"Many don't. That's okay. But the point of the altar call is for people to make a bold statement that they are willing to lay down their burdens at the symbol of God's authority, which is the altar. That is exactly what we need to do tonight."

Simultaneously, all three turned their heads toward the center of the garden. "I think we have our altar," Marie whispered.

Steve took the first step and was immediately joined by Marie and Gavin. They slowly, but assuredly walked toward the stone table in the center of the park. Their altar. Standing silently in front of the table, each of them concealed their thoughts. It was a solemn moment with few immediate answers that would miraculously end this terror.

***

From a distance, the beast had been watching. It had waited for the precise moment to strike when each victim was most vulnerable. But as they stepped up to the table, the beast suddenly knew their intentions. If they were to succeed, the creature knew it would whiter and fade into a memory many would choose to forget. Evil breeds discourse and fear, and the beast thirsted for the suffering of others. Saliva dripped from its jowls as it spied on the trio. The beast leaped from the tree and landed with a solid thud, then righted itself using its powerful appendages. The beast looked directly into the faces of its prey and prowled toward the center of the garden.

***

The ground rumbled slightly underfoot as Gavin, Marie, and Steve stopped directly in front of the stone slab. A simultaneous audible thump indicated this thing of terror was somewhere in the garden with them. Steve looked to his right verifying Gavin and Marie hadn't run off. He needed to know they were going to stand with him. They turned their gaze to Steve, and he silently lifted his hands up from his side and placed them, palms down, on top of their designated altar. Marie and Gavin turned to look at one another, then followed Steve's lead. They brought their hands up and gently rested them on the marble surface. The table was smooth and cool to the touch, like the glass shelf of a refrigerator. Pressing their palms atop the stone, it radiated a sense of peace, betraying the suffocating feeling in the air.

***

It paused briefly and tilted its head from side to side. Curiosity brewed within as the animal had rarely seen its prey stand valiantly in the face of pending doom. Lifting its head, it sniffed the air hoping for the scent of dread emanating from the three humans. The creature merely smelled its own wet fur mixed with blood and dirt.

***

The silence of the moment was broken by the sound of sloshing, water-soaked terra firma giving way under the weight of the beast as it clumsily splashed across the lawn on the opposite side of the table. The group strained to see what they could audibly discern. But the lush scenery and tediously pruned and meticulously shaped shrubbery concealed the beast. They stood in a small clearing encircled by a two-foot stone wall. Only when the beast neared would it leave the concealment of the landscaping.

It paused as it came to a small wall. The beast stepped over the handmade barrier with ease. Looking into their faces, the three stood their ground behind a small table. The beast slowed but continued forward with its pending assault. Each step was deliberate and delicate, knowing it was entering sacred ground.

***

Gavin glanced down, at the six hands and thirty fingers resting on the table. He was wondering how such mediocrity would defeat such ferocity. Steve's chin was raised slightly with his head facing the heavens. His eyes were closed as he silently prayed for power and mercy. Marie was prepared to see the mystery she had valiantly pursued for years. She remained wide-eyed and gazing straight ahead. Waiting. She was the first to see its hideous sight as the beast lost its ability to encroach unseen and moved into the open.

It was immediately evident to Marie that she had never been told stories that contained any degree of first-hand accuracy. In all those tales, the beast had been likened to a wild animal. At best, the depictions had been described as a caricature of a mutated mix of a bear and coyote. She would not have been prepared for the reality of the beast if it were not for Taylor's text to Gavin. Still, there were features the picture on Gavin's phone could not fully capture. Its height was daunting. Even as its legs were bent in two places, it stood at least nine feet tall. The legs and arms moved freely in both directions at the joints. Teeth protruded both horizontally and vertically from its mouth and were jagged. She briefly imagined how efficiently it could eviscerate flesh and bone. It was held up by what looked like two feet at the bottom of each leg. The feet were shaped like the letter 'V' and covered in moppy hair. Still, she could see unkempt claws arched and pushing into the muddy soil. She looked from the ground back to the creature's face. She wanted to look this thing in the eye if it were going to kill her. She was startled to see a vacant mass where one's eyes normally sat. The darkness of its eyeless face pierced into her soul, yet she felt no fear.

Marie's mouth was gaping open with a slight smile forming at each corner. The insignificant grin was not brought on by joy or excitement. She was, however, feeling a sense of finality. Not the finality of life, but confidence she would live past this moment and finally put closure to this mystery.

***

The beast stepped forward with uncertainty in its movements. This was a new sensation for the beast. Uncertainty had never entered its thoughts. It was craving the blood each of these victims would provide. But it sensed power radiating from them second only to the influence Lady Okayo exuded upon its creation. The beast had never feared its game before tonight. The capacity to induce fear and trembling provided motivation to devour its prey. Yet the impact these people had at this moment was different. It was paralyzing and the beast was forced to stop. In its rage at being compelled to pause its attack, the beast opened its mouth to let out its patented scream.

***

By now, Steve and Gavin had heard Marie's subtle and hushed mumbling. Gavin looked up from the table away from their inert hands. Steve lowered his head and opened his eyes. All three watched as the beast's mouth opened wide. They heard it suck in a deep breath, inhaling the night air. After a moment, the mouth remained open, and the air in its lungs reversed as the beast exhaled. The fur surrounding the tongueless void was flapping in the breeze of the beast's breath. Silence continued to envelop them all. Each of the humans had been prepared to endure a blood-curdling scream. None invaded their ears. The only sensation was the heat flowing over them as the beast pushed meaningless air from its lungs.

***

The beast felt a phenomenon like none it had ever experienced. Its vocal cords were silenced. The scream that created fear and trembling became an empty threat. The beast closed its mouth and lowered its head. Mangled fur, wet from the rain and encased with the blood of many, hung limply from its shadowy, empty eye sockets. The beast furrowed its brow, but no human would recognize its action as the mass of hair hid the beast's emotions. It could not display weakness. It knew only how to exhibit confident authority to instigate fear.

***

Without turning to look at his audience, Steve said to Marie and Gavin, "This is our moment. Today we stand with confidence. We face our fears and proclaim truth rather than succumb to our lies. Today, that thing dies. Examine the pain of your heart, soul, and mind. At this table lay down your broken thoughts and stand confidently in the power of who you are. Of whom God created you to be. Marie. Gavin. Steve. You are powerful."

As he included his own name with Marie and Gavin, and spoke it out loud, it forced Steve to analyze his own comments. He had a sudden realization of what he sheltered in a hidden room within the bowels of his brain, and it became brilliantly clear. Standing exposed in this park, vivid memories flooded his mind. Steve lost his foot only two months into deployment. Yet, he had trained for years with the men he proudly served with. His one goal in life had been to serve a long career in the military and it was cut short. Worse still, were the monthly phone calls, emails, and texts he would receive telling him of yet one more brother in arms that had been killed in action. How many funerals could he attend? How many could he officiate? Steve was racked with guilt and depression at his inability to protect his friends. He cursed God at every funeral while putting on a fake smile and reading a Psalm.

With his palms pressed into the stone altar, Steve lay bare his emotions and his pain. He finally recognized he had lied time and again to himself and others. He had clouded the truth and created a false emotional state of mind. Here in the presence of this demon that wanted to devour him, Steve had no more reason to harbor lies. If this whole thing was a farce, he wanted to face his death with a clean slate. He would devour his lies before he was devoured by the creature. He began sobbing uncontrollably. Floods of tears poured out and snot ran down his lips and chin. It was a cleansing of his soul.

Marie and Gavin dared not look at Steve out of fear of joining him with tears and sobbing grunts and noises. Instead, they continued to have a stare-off with the beast. Steve's earlier words impacted each of them and self-examination was pending. As Steve's sobs filled the air, the beast twitched. But it also took a step forward. Marie and Gavin saw the beast inching closer and knew they, too, played a part in destroying this hideous creature. Gavin looked up to the heavens. The sun had not crested the horizon, but its light was beginning to drip into the darkness, creating a purple hue in the sky above. Gazing into the beauty of the heavens, Gavin let out a guttural scream. He had not intended to match the death toll of the beast, but in doing so, he understood the release and relief he felt. Each emotion was wrapped inside a vocal cord and with his yell, those emotions were released into the air around him. The invisible expungement freed himself of each painful memory he had clung to.

With Gavin's cries, the beast reached its arm-like limbs to its head. It pushed into what could presumably be its ears trying to muffle Gavin's cries. What had once been life-filling noise for the beast, was now life-threatening. The screams uttered by Gavin were not filled with fear and despair. Instead, they released hope. This hope brought anguish and pain to the beast which shook its head trying to get the noise to escape its memory. Its palms pushed so tightly inward on its ears, blood seeped out like a sponge being relieved of the water it had dutifully held onto.

Marie was listening and watching. She knew what Steve had asked of each of them. She had even joined in on explaining what needed to be done. Despite knowing what she should do, she could not dig deep enough to pry away the pain embedded within her mind. Like a child clinging to her parents on the first day of kindergarten, her thoughts would not let go. She was scared her failure at this table would give power to her foe. She could do no more. She was tired. Marie gave up and slumped to the ground. She wished the beast would devour her first which would provide time for Gavin and Steve to flee.

***

The beast's head was still being smothered by its arms. The hand-like claws began digging at its ears looking for relief from an itch too far inside one's head to adequately tame. Mimicking Marie, the beast also fell to the ground hoping to gain the relief it erroneously thought she was feeling. It swayed back and forth. Back and forth. Trying to lull itself into a comforting position. The beast felt no relief. Its suffering intensified. It looked at the three pieces of meat on the other side of the table. One was screaming. One was crying. One was balled up on the ground. These were common positions for its prey in years past. But now, at this moment, those very stances were enslaving the beast.

Hoping to overpower its own weakness, the beast used its other appendages to wrap themselves tightly around its body. It cradled itself. An odd sense of comfort encapsulated the beast and it cradled itself tighter. The beast felt warmth from this action and continued to hug with a firm grasp. The warmth overtook the beast. It felt helpless to eliminate this feeling and was something the beast had never experienced. Fearing defeat, the beast quickly stood and extended its appendages away from its body. It stretched its arms forward hoping to grab one of its victims and regain control.

***

From the corner of her blurry, tear-soaked eye, Marie saw the beast rise up. "Run!" she yelled. Still believing she failed the men by her side, she would not budge from her seat on the ground. "Please, run," she whimpered.

At her statement to flee, both Steve and Gavin opened their eyes. The beast was standing at least ten feet tall, just mere feet in front of them. Steve spoke first and emphatically stated, "No! Stand strong!"

Assuming he was inferring to her prostrate position, Marie said again, "I can't stand. I failed us. You need to run. Let it take me."

It was Gavin's turn to set aside his current emotions and speak up. "Marie. You have not failed anyone! Sit. Stand. Lay down. It doesn't matter. Just..." Gavin didn't finish his statement. While speaking he took a quick glance at the beast. Then he silently added, "It's dying."

Steve's eyes were blurry from tears and goop that had escaped his tear ducts and gathered on his lashes. Using the sleeve of his shirt, he wiped his eyes. He had to do this several times to dry the tears and allow focus to be regained. When he was finally able to see clearly, he saw blood oozing out of the sides of the beast's head. Marie was also looking at the beast. She thought she had imagined it earlier, but when it fell on the ground, she assumed it was to attack her at her level. She now realized she had seen blood pouring from where its claws dug into its fur as it rocked back and forth.

"I think it smothered itself so hard, it actually created puncture wounds along its body. It's bleeding out."

The sun was now conquering the eastern skyline. The bright orb had not shown itself in three days. Its light suppressed the darkness, and the beast's wounds were evident. Holes lined its torso and head. Its talons were a brown and red mixture of fresh and drying blood. Confirming its own fate, the beast suddenly fell to the ground. As the three watched the beast writhe on the ground, they silently wondered how they would dispose of its body. Answering the unspoken quandary, the beast began digging at the earth's surface. It voraciously began burrowing a hole. Its grave. When it was satisfied the hole was deep enough, the beast slid into the pit and tried to bury itself with the dirt it had just evacuated from this place. As the three watched, the beast evaporated and disappeared.

October 15, 2013

After the water seeped back into the ground and the original landscape returned, it was evident the process to fully clean was going to take months or years. Once people returned to their homes, they saw the true damage of what Mother Nature can unleash. Gavin went from one location to the next speaking with homeowners as he documented their incredible stories. Basements filled with mud. Family photo albums where each picture had to be carefully pulled from the pages and left in the sun to dry. Dumpster upon dumpster filled with memories and loss. The stories went on and on.

The most powerful narratives were the connections being made between those who lost so much and those who faced no loss and felt the need to help. Donations poured in providing relief via places to stay and money to recoup some of the losses. Gavin could hardly stay abreast of all the many gifts received by donors both near and far. Despite the loss of many pets, presumably to the tides of the river, no mention was made of a great and powerful beast roaming the land. Gavin would prod those he interviewed, hinting toward something more. No one gave any hint of speculation they suspected more than a horrible ill-timed storm.

The church continued to provide support spiritually, mentally, and physically. Many people volunteered their days off to clean, cook, and stand steadfast by the suffering. Steve set aside the memories of his night in the garden and used that experience to be a better man and a more understanding pastor. He chose to move his congregation away from the spiritual religiosity plaguing too many churches and focus more on the hearts of others. Everyone was accepted. Shame was removed. God is not about highlighting sin, but about lifting all up in love and joy. Steve realized he had lost that joy and was determined to find it again and share it with anyone he could.

Marie captured this historical moment in time via journals and more research. She and Gavin decided to use the stories from those he interviewed, and her knowledge of the region, to write a book about the events of the storm. The trick was to blend the history and reality of what had occurred. The beast was real and a part of history, but that story could not be flippantly shared. She would have to find a way to bring the beast to life while sharing about the devastation of the rising waters. She had to reveal the story of the Beckett Beast under the guise of historical fiction.

Epilogue - June 8, 2014

The Colorado sun was especially intense today, pouring its heat onto Gavin's capped head. Even at 12,000 feet in elevation, cool air had escaped the mountainside. Sweat had effectively pooled inside his clothing which only aided in providing occasional cooling relief as the aspen trees pushed the unseen wind against his body. He equated the slight, yet noticeable, breeze to nature's air conditioner. He was grateful for the chill it brought. Something he had not thought he would ever again appreciate.

Gavin stepped carefully down the sloped hillside. The rocks were small and easily let go of their grasp to the ground below. Each footfall was a challenge to stick to the ground without falling on his butt. Mostly, he failed. His left foot in front of his right slid two feet downhill causing him to lose his balance, for the fourth time on this slope, and fall. He was grateful he wore jeans which provided a bit of extra padding than his running shorts would have given. Gavin decided to forego a fifth attempt to stand. Using his arms and hands for side-to-side balance, he decided to put his weight onto the balls of his feet and slide down the next ten feet or so until the path leveled out again.

"Quitter!" Marie hollered down at him.

"Yeah, wait until you decide the same way down is the best before you call me a quitter. Besides, I like to call it smart risk management. No sense in breaking an arm or leg in the middle of nowhere."

"I did not spend $200 on a pair of boots that list non-stick souls as their main attraction just so I could use my butt as a sled!"

"Um-hmm. Well, we are about to find out how well those boots work. Come on down."

Marie slowly placed her right foot on the sloped surface covered with small rocks and pebbles. The ground below her foot held and she carefully moved her left foot in front of her right. It also grasped the ground below and held tight. Marie looked down at Gavin. "See. Works as advertised!" She held up both her arms in a victory stance. The rocks gave way under her slight movement, and she fell backward. She was able to move her arms from above to behind her and her wrists took the brunt of the fall, followed quickly by her lower back and legs. The slide downhill immediately followed.

Gavin and Marie had been through much worse together. He did not respond with pity for her fall and subsequent slide. He let out a belly laugh as he observed her careen downhill toward him. He was already prepared to stop her forward momentum, placing his right foot against the stump of a tree so he would not follow suit and join in the downward journey. Marie smiled, enjoying the ride pretending she was a kid going down the slide at the park.

Marie slid into Gavin's waiting arms. Her momentum was a bit more than either expected and she slid into him, fully pressing her head into his upper body. He wrapped his arms around her back and held her in an embrace.

"I guess non-slip soul may apply more to a linoleum surface than what we get out here in nature," Marie said. Her words were muffled as she was speaking into Gavin's left shoulder.

"Well, the boots may have held. It was the rocks that had no agreement to stay put."

"True. I guess I'll keep the boots," Marie smiled. Not that she had a choice now to return or discard the protector of her feet.

With a natural pause in their journey, Gavin thought it a good idea to stop for a quick refuel of trail mix and water. "I guess this is as good a place as any to go ahead and take a break. What do you think, Marie? You hungry?"

"Sure. Besides, look behind you."

Gavin turned to take in the scenery. The valley they were descending into still lay another 1,000 feet down in elevation. From this vantage point, he could see the valley floor, the stream running down its center, and the peaks towering on all sides.

"Truly breathtaking. I feel like I'm in the Alps."

"Right?" Marie agreed.

They sat on boulders turned benches and chewed as silently as possible. Neither wanted the sounds of nature to be obscured by their chomping of peanuts and chocolate pieces. As Gavin neared the end of his snack he looked toward Marie. "Where's the map app show us at?"

"You don't have to say 'map app' every time you refer to it, dork. It's just a map. Or an app."

"But the alliteration is so great."

"Again… you are a dork."

"I will give you no arguments there. So, how close are we?" Gavin asked, seeking information that would lead to their destination. Which was the primary reason for their hike today.

"Look across the valley, to the hillside on the left. All the trees are down."

"Yep. So that's where the avalanche hit?"

"It makes sense. Every tree is pointing downhill, toward the stream. Clearly, they were knocked over by a force from above, pushing them down."

Gavin was feeling an internal sense of hesitation to continue their journey. He prodded Marie to see where she was mentally. "And you're sure you want to go down there? It hasn't even been a year since the scare of my life ended. We may be pushing fate here."

"I'm sure. Aren't you? You were all gung-ho last week when we discussed this."

"Events like this seem much more attractive from the security of one's home. Maybe it would help if I knew why you fell to the ground at that marble table and told Steve and me to run."

"Maybe it would help if you told me why you let out such a loud, lonely scream," Marie countered.

"Fair enough. There's no need to go back to that morning and describe our inner secrets. We beat that thing and that is all that matters now. But we don't know what's down there." Gavin's tone trailed off just a bit as he pointed into the valley below.

"But there's so many stories that provide a pretty good picture. And the recent record-breaking avalanche season may provide the answers we need."

The next few minutes were filled with the sound of the aspens and pines whispering with the wind. The patter of tiny feet from the small creatures that scrambled over rocks as Marie and Gavin tossed bits of bread to them was the only other interruption of the quiet mountain air. They needed this time to center and focus. What lay ahead neither could really know. Folly. False leads. Or ferocity. They needed to prepare for it all.

Marie's voice cut into the atmosphere. "Ready?"

"As best as I can be."

Marie and Gavin picked up their packs, made sure they left no trash behind and turned their backs toward the slippery slope they had just slid down. Their focus turned toward the unknown terrain of this mountain ridge that was vacated decades ago by miners who willingly left all gear behind to avoid the terror of the nights. Had it all been a scam to push the gold diggers away? They hoped to soon discover the answer.